I miss you.
I ache for you.
Where did you go?
I would really like to know.
I refuse to believe that with one fateful twist,
You completely ceased to exist.
Sometimes I smell your perfume on the air.
Find myself looking to see if you're there.
Always staring into space,
Missing the vision of your beautiful face.
I crave your kiss.
I can't go on like this.
Nikki.
Nikki.

FINDING *Chase*

By Lacey Weatherford

Moonstruck Media- Arizona

FINDING *Chase*

Copyright © 2011 Lacey Weatherford
ALL RIGHTS RESERVED
ISBN-13: 978-1481124027
ISBN-10: 1481124021

Published by

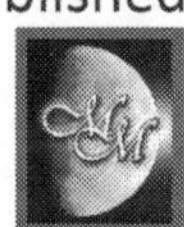

Moonstruck Media - Arizona

Without limiting the rights under copyright reserved above, no part of this publication may be reproduced, stored in or introduced into a retrieval system, or transmitted, in any form, or by any means (electronic, mechanical, photocopying, recording, or otherwise) without the prior written permission of both the copyright owner and the above publisher of this book.

This is a work of fiction. Names, characters, places, brands, media, and incidents are either the product of the author's imagination or are used fictitiously. The author acknowledges the trademarked status and trademark owners of various products referenced in this work of fiction, which have been used without permission. The publication/use of these trademarks is not authorized, associated with, or sponsored by the trademark owners.

Edited by Irene Hunt, Third-Eye Tight Editing Services

This book is also available in ebook format.
http://laceyweatherfordbooks.com.

Acknowledgments

As usual, it takes more than just me to write a book. This project was extremely emotional on many levels, so I'm glad for the opportunity to thank those who've been so crucial in helping me get this developed.

First off, I'd like to thank my best friend, Belinda, for being there when I felt like everything was falling apart around me and I couldn't stop crying. Your advice and giving me ways to pull myself together allowed this story could continue on. Without you, I'm not sure if this book would've ever been finished. I appreciate that you've decided to accept the challenge of having a sensitive basket case of a friend like me.

Second, I'd like to thank my wonderful husband, James, for continually being my sounding board. Thanks for backing up the things Belinda tells me and being a support to me no matter how badly my mood swings shift. I love you!

Third, thanks to my fabulous editor Irene. You do such an amazing job helping to put the fine polish on my projects and making them shine. I also want to thank you for the time you invested in listening to my story development and helping me to think outside the box that is my head. I'm so grateful to have you in my life and I love your dedication to everything.

And last, but definitely not least, thanks to my readers—without you there's no reason to write. I appreciate the support I've received from all of you!

Hugs and Kisses!

Lacey

Dedication

For my readers who begged me to please give them the rest of Chase's story. This book is for you.

~

And for Chase, the muse who made my favorite character burst to life inside my head.

Part One

~Chapter One~

Just because I'd given her my vow, didn't mean I'd stopped thinking about doing it.

I looked through the windshield at the serene view ahead—one which belied the inner turmoil boiling inside me—and slammed my foot against the gas pedal. The engine roared, and the truck shook as it vibrated.

My hand slid closer to the gearshift. All I had to do was take it out of park, and it would go sailing off the edge of the cliff in front of me.

So easy.

I glanced down, my gaze settling on the state championship football ring on my finger. If it hadn't been for her, I would've never earned it.

"Stop looking at the past," Nikki's voice echoed in my head for the millionth time. *"Look to the future."*

I released the gas pedal and hung my head in remorse.

"I wasn't really going to do it," I said with a sigh, answering as if she were sitting next to me. Sometimes I still wanted to, but I'd let her down enough. I wouldn't break my word.

As usual, she didn't reply, but I guessed that was to be expected since she was dead.

My mind drifted over the memories of our too short relationship. She was constantly in my thoughts, which was difficult to deal with since I'd banned myself from coping in my preferred way—with drugs and alcohol.

I'd kept that promise as well, attending group

sessions and learning how to avoid falling back into those patterns and habits. While I had never truly been addicted to anything, I could see I'd definitely been headed in that direction. The things I'd learned to recognize about myself helped me have better control, but at the same time, caused added irritation. In becoming and staying clean, I found myself overwhelmed with memories of both her and my dad. Things I'd refused to dwell on for so long were always right at the surface.

Sighing, I carefully put my truck into reverse and backed away from my precarious position, turning in the direction of the ranch. I'd really grown to love the place. It had been some of the best therapy available. I kept busy with sports, then came home and threw myself into my chores and homework. Anything I could do to exhaust my mind was beneficial; otherwise, I couldn't go to sleep at night.

My hard work paid off, though. I'd graduated from high school with almost straight A's, and after being named State Football Player of the Year in my division, I had my pick of colleges knocking at my door.

My family and friends were excited to see my sports career continue. They couldn't understand why I hedged on picking a school, not realizing my thoughts dwelled on Nikki. This was when she and I had planned on starting our life together. Every time I looked at the list of places offering scholarships, all I could think of was our conversations and how excited we were to see where we would end up.

I'd met with a few recruiters at the beginning of the summer and even made trips to check out some of the schools' programs. In the end, I decided to keep things close. One of my choices was Arizona State University, which would not only allow me to stay near my family and easily make trips home on free weekends, but would also give me the opportunity of attending school with several people from my core group of friends.

I had to laugh at myself. I remembered being anxious to leave this place when I first arrived. Now I was deliberately staying close, so I could be here more often. My family was thrilled with my choice—happy they were relevant in my decision. I wondered if they realized they'd become my anchors, the people who kept me stable. I didn't think they understood how much I needed them.

Oh, I could put on a good show of moving on when I needed to. There had come a point when I felt if I got condolences from another person, my head might explode. In fact, there were days I could have gone postal on some of those well-meaning people. I knew they were trying to help because I was sad, so I did my best to fake happy when I was out and about. It made people back off a bit.

There was only one place I could go and truly let down and be myself. That's when I was at Nikki's house. I often spent my free evenings with her family, cuddling on the couch with Timmy and Clara after eating a great dinner her mom, Justine, had prepared. I fit in there because they were mourning the same way I was. No one expected me to be chipper and happy all the time because they weren't either.

Nikki's room still remained exactly the way it was when she died. Her mom kept it closed and no one went in anymore. It hurt too badly to look at it, but I don't think any of us were ready to let her go yet. I couldn't count the times I'd stopped in the hall and rested my hand on the knob as I leaned against the door, wishing I could open it and find her sitting on the other side like I had all those times in the past.

I often wondered if perhaps she was still around somewhere, like a guardian angel. I couldn't imagine her being anything other than an angel, because that's what she'd been when she was alive.

One thing I was positively sure of, was I didn't want to date anymore. There was no way I was willing to risk being close to someone again. It was too painful to lose them. There was also the fact I didn't think there was another soul in the world who would ever be able to replace Nikki in my heart. I had my family and my few best friends. They were all I needed. I wasn't letting anyone new get close.

I parked my truck in front of the big, white ranch house and grabbed the bags of groceries I'd purchased from the back seat. I found Brett sitting on the porch swing.

"Where have you been?" he asked as I approached. "I've been waiting for almost an hour. Not that I'm complaining. Your grandma felt the need to feed me while you were gone." He smiled.

"I took the scenic route home."

"I called your phone, and it went straight to message." Brett hopped up to open the door.

"Hmm, I must've forgotten to turn it back on after I charged it."

"Everything okay?" He scrutinized me for a second, always able to read my moods.

"I'll be fine. Just thinking things over."

He didn't reply as we walked into the kitchen to give Grandma Caroline her purchases.

"There you are!" She smiled as if she'd missed me incredibly in the two hours I'd been gone. She brushed her hands on her apron. "What took you so long?"

"He took the scenic route," Brett explained.

"Ah." She didn't press any further, and I wonder whether or not I should be irritated a simple statement like that could speak volumes to everyone.

I placed the bags on the counter, but Grandma

ignored them, wrapping her arms around me instead.

"I love you, Chase."

"Love you too," I replied hugging her back. "Is there anything else you want me to do?"

"No." She released me and began unloading the bags. "Brett's here to help you with your things now. I know you have a lot to pack."

"Yeah. Let me know if you need me for anything." I left the room, Brett following after, and the two of us made our way up the stairs toward the living quarters for my mom and me.

We were both leaving. Mom was getting married to her fiancé, Greg Stanton, at the end of the summer, and she was moving into his huge house.

Grandpa and Grandma had offered to let me keep my room here, and I'd taken them up on it. The ranch had become my home, and I didn't want to leave. Plus, I thought it would seem strange to come visit and stay at Greg's when this is where I really wanted to be.

"Do you ever take a minute to sit down and relax anymore?" Brett asked.

I snorted in reply.

"Seriously. You need to take a breather once in a while. You're working yourself to the bone. I hope you're going to take a bit of time off to enjoy the parties and stuff at school. I doubt you even remember what a party is."

I glanced at him. "I won't be attending any parties."

He laughed. "Of course you will. Everyone knows ASU is one of the biggest party schools in America."

"I'm serious. I won't be going to any. I need to concentrate on my classes and football practice, so I can meet the requirements for my scholarship." I went over and tapped on the glass fishbowl beside my bed. "Hey, Turk. How ya doing?"

"That's bull, and you know it. I have the same

amount of classes, and I'm walking on to the football team. If I have time to go to a party, then so do you. Heck, the football team probably has some of the biggest partiers on it."

I dropped a few flakes of food in Turk's bowl. "And what's at those parties, Brett? Alcohol? Drugs? Those are the two things I went to therapy to get control of."

"You don't have to drink or do drugs to have a good time. I was thinking it would be a nice way for us to meet new people."

I could see he wasn't going to let this go.

"I assume by people, you mean girls. Won't *your* girlfriend, Tana, have a problem with that? Especially since she's attending ASU, to be with you and your sister, Brittney?"

He was silent.

"Oh, I see. You don't want to meet anyone—you want me to. Forget about it now, because it's not going to happen." Feeling frustrated, I walked to my closet and pulled out my luggage and some flattened boxes.

Brett huffed. "Dude, you can't be celibate forever."

"Yeah? Watch me." I started folding and taping the boxes together.

"You're seriously telling me you have no desire for any kind of a relationship with any girl for the rest of your life?"

I spun around to face him. "No, I'm telling you I only want to be with *one* girl, and *she's* not available anymore. I'm telling you I'm not willing to risk putting myself through the trauma I've been through with Nikki ever again. And I'm asking you, as my best friend, to understand and respect that!"

He stood in silence, staring while he clenched his jaw. "I'm sorry for what you've lost, Chase, but I have to say that sounds like a long, lonely life. You have so much you could offer someone."

I took a deep breath and ran a hand through my hair, turning back to the boxes I was assembling. "I don't want anyone else. I love Nikki."

"We all do," Brett said softly. "And I know she loved you more than anything, but it's been months now. I think she'd want you to be happy."

The tears crept into my eyes, and I blinked them away before I spoke. "She's not here to say what she wants, and this conversation is over."

~Chapter Two~

"I can have Greg do that, Chase. You don't need to bother with it right now."

"It's not a hardship, Mom. Really." I grabbed another box from her room and carried it down to my truck.

Her hands were on her hips, and she was glaring when I returned.

"You're working too much—all the time lately. Take a break, and go hang out with your friends before you leave."

I laughed. "Most of my friends are going with me. Seriously, I'd rather be helping you." I wrapped my arms around her shoulders and rested my chin on the top of her head. "Why are you always trying to get rid of me? Am I that much of a thorn in your side still?"

She hugged me tightly. "I don't ever want to be rid of you. I simply want you to have some fun for a change. And quit talking about leaving, or I'm going to start crying. I'm going to miss you so badly."

"You're not even going to notice I'm gone," I teased. "I know how it'll be . . . you and Greg, alone in a big old house." I shuddered and she laughed, shoving me away.

"Just for that, I'm going to let you haul all these boxes over there."

"I was going to do it anyway." I grinned as I went to get another one.

It wasn't long until I had everything she'd packed in the back of the truck. I shut the tailgate firmly and faced her. "Anything else you need me to take?"

She shook her head. "No. I'll need the stuff that's

left here until after the wedding. This place is going to look bare after you take most of the furniture with you."

"Well, you know I'd be happy to stay longer if I could. I'll be back every weekend, though, until school starts."

"I'm excited for you to start practicing with the team. I'm sure you'll be wowing them in no time at all."

I shook my head. "Don't hold your breath, Mom. I might be the top dog around here, but I'll be the little guy on the totem pole there. I'll be lucky if the coaches even know my name."

"Whatever. They know who you are, otherwise they wouldn't have offered you a scholarship. Everyone who knows anything about football in Arizona knows who Chase Walker is."

I laughed again and climbed inside my truck. "We'll see about that."

Leaning against the tree, I sighed heavily and wished I could ease the terrible ache in my heart. No one knew about this secret ritual of mine—it was something I'd chosen to keep between Nikki and me. I was going to miss it once I went away. Sometimes it was the only peace I could find—the only place I allowed myself to break down and really feel.

I thought back to how I'd initially told myself I wasn't ever going to come here again, but after about a week I couldn't stand being away. I needed to be as close to her as I could. I hadn't missed a week since.

"I'm moving away to the valley tomorrow. Football practice is starting."

I stared at the beautiful granite headstone which graced her resting place. Her gorgeous senior picture, taken a few days before the accident, was embedded in it. She looked so alive—so vibrant. I liked to imagine she was here, listening and smiling at me when I came to talk.

"I'll be back to see you every weekend until school starts. Then I'll have games on Saturdays, and I won't be able to come as often until the season is over."

I paused and looked down at the ground. Pulling up a few blades of grass, I twirled them between my fingers.

"I promise I won't forget you," I said, continuing my one-sided conversation. "I'll think about you every day, and hopefully you'll be out there somewhere watching over me. Sometimes it's the only thing that keeps me sane . . . hoping wherever you are, you can see me, and you aren't as lonely as I am."

I didn't know how to close and heal this wound. I needed her help to mend it.

"Nikki, I'm having a hard time. This was when we'd planned on starting our lives together. I can't see past the fact I'll be leaving you here while I go on. I swear I've tried to move past this, but I can't seem to. My heart is stuck with you. When you died, my hopes and dreams died with you—I'm simply going through the motions. I look around and see everyone continuing on like they don't realize the sun has quit shining. Everything seems dark and negative now. I'm not myself anymore. I might appear the same on the outside, but inside . . . inside I'm hollow. How do I fix that? How do I go forward when all I want is to be with you? How do I carry on when it's my fault you're lying here?"

The panic I repeatedly fought against began to rise inside me. I hated facing something I couldn't control. It left me feeling completely helpless, knowing *nothing* I did would ever change the outcome. This was my life now. I was being forced to travel a road I never wanted to take in the first place. It made me incredibly angry at everything. Emotions tumbled and churned, welling up so swiftly I thought I might start screaming.

Jumping to my feet, I dropped the blades of grass and placed a hand on her headstone, gripping it tightly. "I've got to go, Nikki. I'm sorry I'm never strong enough to stay here very long. I can't take it. It eats me up." My knuckles were turning white, and I released the granite piece and stepped away. "I love you."

Clenching my fists beside me, I headed toward my truck. I felt the need to pummel something. I was glad football was starting, so I had the excuse to pour this emotion into something very physical. I needed something—anything—to ease the frustration.

"Good heavens, boy! What're you up to?" Grandpa Warren's voice came from the doorway, and I glanced in his direction before returning to work.

"I thought I'd restack the hay bales for you. They looked sloppy, and this one row was pretty close to the outside wall. I noticed sometimes water leaks under right there. I didn't want it to get ruined if it rained." I tossed another bale on top of the bottom one before climbing up the stack and hefting it higher, moving towards the upper part of the pile.

"Chase, I can take care of this. You've got a house full of people here for your goodbye party tonight. You need to come inside."

Pausing, I wiped my arm across my sweaty brow and glanced in the direction of the house. "I don't really feel like partying. Maybe you can make excuses for me? I'll grab some leftovers when I come in later." I gave a pleading, hopeful look as he stared, his lips pursed.

"Son, come sit with me for a spell." He waved his hand toward some of the bales on the ground.

Sighing, I finished stacking the one I'd been moving and climbed down. I sat beside him, my elbows resting against my knees.

"You've got to be one of the best kids I know." He clapped me on the back. "I may have had my doubts in the beginning, but I don't think I've ever seen a guy your age work as hard as you."

This was high praise coming from him. "Thanks," I mumbled. "I'm just trying to help out."

"I have to say, I don't like it one bit."

His words threw me.

"What?" I glanced up, confused. I thought he appreciated my help.

"You've got your whole life to work yourself to the bone, Chase. You need to enjoy being a kid. Go be with your friends–laugh, be silly, do some crazy things. Hang with the guys for a while, or try dating again. There are some very pretty girls who'd love to find a handsome guy like you paying them attention."

I clenched my jaw, grinding my teeth together. "I can't do that." I got up and grabbed another bale.

"What do you think Nikki would say about how you're behaving?"

Hearing her name made me feel like I'd been sucker punched in the gut. I dropped the hay. "Don't go there. Please, Grandpa. It still hurts too much." I struggled to maintain my composure.

"I had a dog once that got tangled in a loose barbed wire fence. His name was Barley."

Wait. We're talking about dogs now?

"He cut himself real good on his hind leg. I helped him get free, but he ran off before I could put any salve on the wound and dress it proper. He wandered around the edges of the property, limping, but whenever I'd come after him, he'd hightail it away before I could catch him. Finally, one day I found him laying in the field over yonder. His leg was swollen real bad, and I could tell he had a pretty serious infection going on. I knew if I didn't cut him open and drain it, he was going to die, so I pulled out my pocketknife and sliced into it. Ole Barley, he howled like the dickens and even nipped at me pretty sharply. Green smelly puss shot from that thing, though, and I knew he had to feel a lot better getting rid of the pressure. I carried him to the house and cleaned the wound as best I could. It was touch and go for a while, but finally his leg started healing, and he made a full recovery. Barley and I were pretty close after that. He was a good dog."

I folded my arms. "Is there a point to this story?"

He stood and walked in front of me. "The point is, sometimes you've got to lance your wounds, and let all the infection and poison pour out of your soul so it doesn't eat you alive from the inside out. Sometimes we fail to see there are people around us who love us, and they are waiting to help, but we don't let them. Instead, we choose to let things fester, going off on our own—licking wounds as we try to heal ourselves." He put his hands on my shoulders. "Don't let this happen to you, Chase."

I blinked back the tears which threatened and looked away. I knew what he was saying, but I couldn't give in. It was too hard—too much. "I can't let it out," I whispered. "It's . . . too strong."

"I've watched you for months now. Every time those emotions of yours bubble to the surface, you stamp 'em back down inside and let 'em fester even longer. It's not healthy what you're doing. You've been through hell. You've proven the kind of man you are. It's okay to cry." He pulled me to him, hugging tightly. "It's okay to cry," he emphasized again. "I want you to know you aren't alone, son. I love you."

Despite my resolve, his words sunk deep to my core. I struggled against it with everything I had, but I couldn't hold it together. The dam broke, and I clutched the back of his shirt in both of my fists, suddenly overwhelmed with great gulping sobs. I wanted to stop, but I couldn't fight it anymore. I didn't care if I looked foolish because I knew he was right. I'd been in agony, feeling like I had nowhere to turn. I didn't know how to express what was happening inside, so I kept it bottled up the best I could, letting off just enough steam every now and then to keep the pot from exploding. It was more than I could bear.

"I love her, Grandpa," I cried, my words sounding foreign and choked. "I really love her. I don't know how to live without her. I don't want to live without her."

He didn't offer me any words of wisdom, instead holding me as I wept in his arms. I had no idea how long we stood there—I only knew my heart was breaking.

"Warren?" I heard Grandma Caroline's voice come from outside, and she appeared in the doorway, stopping short when she saw the two of us. She placed her hand over her heart, and I saw tears in her eyes.

"We'll be there soon," Grandpa said without moving. "Tell everyone we had to finish some things up first.'

She nodded, blowing me a kiss before she walked away. Grandpa released me, and I stepped backward, lifting my hands to dry my face.

"I want you do something for me," he said, carefully watching me.

"What's that?"

"I want you to do one fun thing every day. I don't want you to feel guilty about it. Give yourself permission to let go once in a while. Do it for your old gramps if you have to. I can't send you away to school without knowing you'll promise to do this."

I slipped my hands into my pockets, toeing some loose hay on the floor with my boot. "I'll try." I swallowed hard, attempting to push past the knot in my throat.

"Try hard, because I'm gonna ask you every week to tell me what you did. Okay? Take small baby steps to begin with. Can you do that for me?"

I nodded, not able to speak.

He draped his arm around my shoulder. "Come on. We'll sneak you in the back way, so you can shower and get cleaned up for dinner. It's time for you to rejoin your family and friends."

~Chapter Three~

Staring at myself in the mirror, I quickly ran a comb through my dark, towel-dried hair before deeming myself presentable enough to join the others downstairs. Ironically, Grandpa's advice had helped. I did feel a bit better, not that my problems were any different. I sighed and attempted to brush my moody thoughts from my head. It was time to put on my "I'm okay" demeanor as best I could and play a different role.

Laughter rose up the stairs to greet me as I descended, and I picked my mom's voice out above them all. I loved the sound of it. Knowing she was happy brought a small smile to my own lips as I rounded the corner into the kitchen. She was leaning against the counter, and her eyes sparkled as she listened to a story Grandpa was telling. Her fiancé, Greg, had his arm wrapped around her, love plainly written on his face as he stared at her. I paused and watched for a moment—she was so beautiful.

She turned and saw me, and her face lit up even brighter. "There he is!" she said, coming to give me a hug, and the focus of the room shifted in my direction. "Are you all right?" she whispered into my ear.

"Yeah, everything's chill," I replied as I hugged her in return. I released her and bobbed my head toward the others who were crowded around the giant table in the dining area. "Hey everyone."

Brett gave me a nod and his girlfriend, Tana, stood to give me a hug. Before I could reach her, however, I was bowled over by Timmy and Clara, who attacked me, sliding down around my knees, capturing me. I laughed and snatched them up, carrying one under each arm.

"Who let these two terrors in here?" I questioned as they giggled, trying to hang on. "I'm pretty sure I didn't invite them."

"Aunt Tori did!" Clara squealed, calling my mom by the pet name they'd given her.

I grinned at their mom, Justine. "I don't think I gave Aunt Tori permission to do that." I wiggled my fingers against their sides, tickling them, and they screamed as I swung them around.

"Stop!" Timmy laughed. "It tickles!"

"That's the whole point isn't it?" I carefully let them slide to their feet before squatting to give them each a hug. "Thanks for coming to see me," I said, ruffling their hair.

Clara's smile slid from her face. "I don't want you to move away." She threw her arms around my neck.

I held her tight. "I'll come visit as often as I can."

She let go and stared skeptically. "Pinky promise?" She held her little finger out.

"Pinky promise," I replied, wrapping mine around hers. I winked and released her.

My gaze swept around the table at everyone else, and I gave a wave to Brett's sister, Brittney, and also to my good friends Chad and Wes. "Thanks for coming."

"Wouldn't miss it, man," Chad replied.

"He's not here for you," Wes added. "He's here for your grandma's cooking."

I grinned. "I don't blame him. Grandma's the best cook around."

"I agree! Let's eat!" Grandpa said, and I found a seat at the table as everyone began passing the food around.

"Personally, I think you should move with us to the

valley, Mrs. Johnson," Brett said. "You can cook for Chase and me every day. It would help a lot."

Grandma laughed. "You don't need an old lady like me hanging around cramping your style."

"You could never cramp anyone's style," I said as I took a bite of the pasta she'd made.

She beamed. "And that kind of sucking up is exactly what's going to get you fresh cookies in the morning."

"Right on!" I grinned and looked at Brett, Tana, and Brittney. "I don't know about you, but I'll be having a party in my pickup on the way to Tempe."

"I think I'll ride with Chase," Brittney said with a laugh.

"That's not fair," Brett complained, elbowing his sister. "If Tana and I have to go without cookies, so do you."

"It's totally fair," I replied. "Why should she have to watch the two of you mauling each other, when she can ride with me *and* have cookies? It's a no brainer." I glanced at Brittney and winked. "Stick with me, Britt. I got your back."

She laughed and poked her tongue at Brett. "I win!"

Tana smiled. "Or did you? We now have the car to ourselves."

"Ah, to be young and headed off to college again," Justine spoke up. "I miss those days."

"I know, right?" my mom said. "I'd give anything to have the energy I had back then."

"Those days!" Grandpa broke in. "Quit talking like that. You're going to make me feel like I'm an old man."

"You'll never be old, Daddy." Mom reached over and squeezed his hand.

"I can attest to that," my grandma added, waggling her eyebrows.

I groaned loudly. "This conversation just got scary. New subject, please, before we're all scarred for life."

Everyone laughed.

"When's your first practice?" Greg asked me, and I was relieved. Football should be a safe conversation.

"The day after tomorrow, but it's more of a meet and greet, go through the rules, get our gear kind of thing. I don't know if we will actually start any of our training until the next day."

"Well, work hard. Hopefully someone will recognize you've got talent."

"I'll do my best," I replied. I knew I had a lot to prove when I got there, though. Things wouldn't come nearly as easy as they did for me here.

I parked outside Brett's house early in the morning. I'd kept the goodbyes this morning as brief as possible. There was no sense in having a bunch of sadness at parting when I'd be returning often.

Nikki's mom and the kids had actually been the hardest. Clara cried and Timmy clung to me like he was never going to see me again. I had to keep reassuring them I'd come home as much as possible.

Justine held me for several long moments. "Please be careful," she whispered. "You know you're like my own child now."

"I'll be careful," I promised. She looked so much like Nikki, especially now she'd grown her hair out a bit. For one brief second I tried to imagine it was really Nikki in my arms instead. Sometimes it was still hard for me to look at her.

A knock on my window brought me out of my musings. Brett was standing there, and I popped the door open.

"You gonna sit there all day, or are we gonna get this thing loaded up? Let's get out of here." He grinned.

"Let's do it. Do you have Tana and Brittney's things packed already?" I asked surveying the items I could see stacked on the porch.

"Yeah. My dad helped me load my truck with their stuff last night. All that's left is my bed and a few boxes to go in yours."

"Oh, before I forget. My grandma sent these for you. They're fresh from the oven."

His grin widened as I handed him the giant plastic bag full of chocolate chip cookies. "I knew she wouldn't be that mean. No way can your car be the only one with goodies in it."

"Yeah, she's too kind hearted."

"Morning, Chase," Brittney's voice interrupted as she came down the steps.

"Hey. How are you today?" I left my pickup and gave her a hug.

"Look, Britt," Brett said, holding up the treats. "His grandma sent cookies for our car too. What's your excuse for not riding with Tana and me now?"

"She doesn't need an excuse," I interjected. "Everyone knows I'm way cooler than you. That should be reason enough."

Brett elbowed me, and Brittney laughed. "Whatever," he said. "Twin brother trumps football stud every time, right Brittney?"

She appeared to ponder this carefully, glancing between us.

"I have two different kinds of cookies in my truck," I added.

"Sorry, bro. I'm going with the football stud," she replied quickly, and I laughed as Brett shook his head in defeat.

"She just wants you for your cookies, man."

I narrowed my eyes at her. "Is that true?"

She gave me a wide, innocent look. "Of course not. You're one of *my* best friends too. Why should Brett get to do everything with you by himself? Today is my turn." She poked her tongue at him.

"She does have a point there." I glanced at Brett with a sly smile. "You do hog me."

He grabbed me around the shoulders with one arm. "That's because I loooove you, bro." He made grossly distorted kissing lips angling toward my cheek, and I shoved him away, laughing.

"You're sick, dude. Let's get your stuff, so we can get going. Is Tana meeting us here?" I really hoped so. I hated driving to her place and passing the spot of Nikki's accident.

"Yeah, her mom is bringing her by right now."

We headed toward the house, and I noticed Brittney wasn't with us. I glanced around and found her leaning into my truck, digging a cookie from the bag. Brett paused to see what I was looking at and shook his head.

"I warned you."

Brittney glanced up and caught us staring. "What?" she asked, as she took a bite and sighed.

"Nothing," I replied, smiling. "I know the lure of Grandma's baking."

The sound of a car pulling into the driveway alerted us to Tana's arrival, and Brett left to greet her. I grabbed a box, stacked it on top of another one and started hauling his things to my truck. A small smile slipped across my lips. I was glad we were doing this together. It would be fun for Brett and me to be neighbors with the girls in our new apartment complex. A momentary stab of sadness followed. These girls were Nikki's two best friends. She would've been my neighbor too.

~Chapter Four~

"You gonna save me any of those?" I asked Brittney. "What is that now? Four?"

She rolled her eyes as she licked her fingers. "It's not like you don't have two dozen on the seat next to you. Are you really going to miss four?"

I grinned. "No. I just like messing with you."

"Why?" She looked truly puzzled.

"Because you make it so easy. You know Brett and I sit around and think of ways we can torment you, don't you?"

"I do. That's why I try to ignore most things the two of you say." She took another cookie from the bag. "I was done, but I'm going to eat one more to spite you."

Laughing, I reached for another myself. "Go right ahead. I'm not the one who'll be in the gym complaining about it later."

She stared at her dessert. "You're right. Do you want this?"

"I was kidding." I shook my head. "You couldn't get fat if you tried."

"That's what you think." She frowned a little. "Matt's always telling me how fat I am."

"Then you should definitely eat the cookie because Matt's a douche. I never could figure out how you ended up with such a jerk. Why do you stay with him?"

"He's not that bad." She stared out the window but didn't defend him anymore.

"If he's so wonderful, why isn't he here helping you move today?"

She shrugged. "I guess he figured you and Brett had it covered."

"Have you seen him since he moved down there?"

She shook her head. "No. He said he was too busy to make the trip home. He calls almost every day, though."

"*Almost* every day?" I snorted. "Dump him, Britt. He's not worth your time. Any guy who doesn't try to get in touch with you every day isn't as into you as he should be."

She bit her lip and looked at me, tiny lines creasing between her brows. "He calls everyday when we're in the same town."

I was skeptical. "And what kinds of things does he say to you? Is there a romantic under the idiot?" I'd never been quiet about my opinion of Matt.

"No, not really. He usually wants to know what I'm wearing."

"Excuse me? What you're wearing? Oh, wait. This isn't about some sexy booty call, is it? If so, I don't want to hear anymore."

She shrugged, and started examining one of her hands. "It's not anything like that. Sometimes he doesn't like the clothes I choose."

I was dumbfounded for a moment as I tried to process this. "Are you saying he *calls* you and tells you what to *wear*?"

She didn't answer.

"Come on! You've got to be kidding me! Please don't tell me you actually listen to this jerk." I paused, and when she didn't say anything I continued on, my eyes widening as I stared at her incredulously. "You've actually changed your clothes for him?"

"He *is* my boyfriend. I should look nice for him. If it means I have to change a few times to please him . . . never mind. You don't understand," she responded quietly.

"You're right. I don't. And I'm betting you don't either. Have you looked at yourself in a mirror, Britt? You're gorgeous—stunning even. Any guy you're dating should feel like the luckiest person in the world to have you on his arm. I don't care if you're walking around wearing a paper bag."

She half laughed, half snorted. "Whatever, Chase."

"I'm totally serious. I've always thought you were one of the prettiest girls I've ever seen. Don't let some jerk bully you around and make you feel less than you are. I'm not saying this to be mean, or because I don't like him." I glanced back to the road. "But I am a guy, and I know what I'm talking about. When I was with Nikki . . . ," I trailed off, realizing what I'd said.

"You two were perfect for each other," she replied softly. "I'll never forget how crazy she was about you. She spoke of you nonstop."

"Really?" My interest was piqued as she successfully diverted my focus. I craved hearing more. "What did she say?"

"You know, the usual . . . how much she loved you, how amazing you are, did we see your arms in the shirt you wore . . that kind of stuff."

I chuckled. "My arms?"

"She had a serious thing for your biceps. She said they were so strong, and she loved the feel of them when you held her."

"Hmmm . . . interesting. I never knew she noticed. What else did she tell you?" I wanted to hear everything she could tell me.

"Well, there was this one day . . . oh, never mind. I can't tell you about it."

Worry shot through me. Was there something about Nikki I didn't know?

"Why can't you?" I asked, determined to find out

what it was.

"She swore Tana and me to secrecy. She said she'd die . . . ." she paused uncomfortably, "said she'd die if you found out. I'm sorry. That was a poor choice of words."

"Don't feel bad. Tell me what it was," I encouraged.

"Chase, I'm feeling like this might not be the best thing to talk about right now. I know you've struggled, and I don't want to say anything that would hurt your feelings."

I glanced over. "Now you're scaring me. I have these horrible things running through my mind now. Pull off the Band-aid fast, and tell me."

"She went and bought a bunch of bridal magazines and made us look at dresses with her while she planned her dream wedding, with you as the groom, of course."

"Honestly? She talked about marrying me?" I couldn't help my initial grin, but it was quickly followed by the realization it was a wedding that would never happen.

She laid her hand on my shoulder and squeezed slightly. "I'm sorry. Now you know why I didn't want to tell you."

"No, it's okay, really." I rubbed a hand over my face. "I have to say, it's nice to hear some new things about her. Everyone is super sensitive about the subject around me—not that I make it easy—but I find myself missing being able to talk to people about her. I'm tired of hearing everyone is sorry she's dead. I keep getting these sympathetic looks and condolences. Lying in a casket six feet under isn't the way I want to remember her. I want to remember her *alive* and *vibrant*. That was *my* Nikki—so extremely full of life. *Those* are the stories I want to hear. I miss her."

Brittney dropped her hand from my shoulder and was silent for a moment. "I'm sorry, Chase. I had no idea you felt that way. We've been trying not to talk about her because we didn't want to hurt you."

"I know, but having all of you avoid the subject has left me alone in a really dark place. I'm not doing very well by myself."

"What can I do?" she asked, concerned. "We all love you—you know that—we'd do anything to help you through this."

"Talk to me like you used too. No more walking around on egg shells. I hate when we are having a good time together and someone brings up Nikki, and it gets quiet, and everyone looks at me. I want things to be normal—like they were before she died. We used to joke around and razz each other about everything. Quit treating me like I'm so fragile I'm gonna break."

"We did think you were going to break for a while. It was scary."

I glanced over. "What do you mean?"

"We thought you were suicidal. Brett and I were worried you might do something to hurt yourself." She paused and waited. When I didn't reply, she continued. "Were we right? Did you want to die?"

I snorted. "Every single day. I'd even started planning how I'd do it."

She closed her eyes, as if what I was telling her was too painful to hear. "Why didn't you?"

"Her mom let me read her journal. There was a letter to me in there. She went on and on about how much she loved me, how I was amazing and wonderful." I recalled her words perfectly—I'd reread them so many times. "She told me to never give up—she was proud of me and my accomplishments. After that, I felt like I would be letting her down—if I kill myself, I'm not the guy she thought I was. Maybe it's silly, but I don't want to disappoint her anymore than I have."

"It's not silly, and I think she must be proud of

you."

I sighed, scanning the view in front of us before gazing up at the sky for a moment. "You think she's still out there somewhere?"

"I do, and she's probably watching over you every second. She loved you a lot."

The emotion was getting too thick again, and I could feel the panic starting to rise. "Tell me something happy about her," I pleaded. I needed to change the solemn mood.

"Ok. Let me think." She leaned against the headrest. "From any time?"

"Sure." I just wanted her to talk.

"Well, Tana has known her longer, of course, so they've always been the best of best friends. They adopted me later on when I moved to Silver Creek in middle school. Tana didn't really care for me at first, because one of the boys she liked started paying attention to me. She was determined to give me the cold shoulder, but Nikki kept inviting me to do stuff with them. It was a little awkward at first, but eventually Tana warmed up."

"Did you steal her guy?" I asked with a snicker.

"Yes, I did, but it didn't matter because soon she only had eyes for Brett. Did you know they were a couple back then too?"

"Yeah, he told me. Nikki and I conspired to set them up again." Thinking about it made me smile.

"It doesn't surprise me. Nikki was probably one of the most incurable romantics I know." She laughed. "She always wanted her white knight to come in and sweep her off her feet."

I grimaced. "And she got me instead."

She punched me in the shoulder. "Whatever! You were totally her white knight."

I scoffed, sending her an offended look. "Are you

saying I can't tan? I totally can. Look at these arms—brown."

She giggled. "You know what I mean. You were perfect for her. Besides, I don't think farmer tans count as real tans."

"Oh, I'm officially wounded! You did not just say I have a farmer tan!"

"If the shoe fits . . . ," she trailed off, clearly challenging me.

I lifted the hem of my shirt, displaying my brown stomach, making sure I flexed too, so she could clearly see my abs. "This is *not* a farmer tan."

Her eyes widened, and she stared for a second before looking quickly away. "Impressive," she said, her face flushing with color. "Put your shirt down, Walker. There's no need for nudity to prove your point."

I dropped it back in place. There was suddenly a weird tension, and I wasn't entirely sure I liked it. I cleared my throat. "So you admit you're wrong?" I asked, trying to move past the awkwardness.

Her face colored again, and she turned her head farther away, staring through the window at the scenery. "Yes," she said quietly. "You look very nice."

"Nice." I cringed. "That word has to be like the kiss of death or something. It's been my experience, whenever girls use *nice*, it's not a good thing."

She locked eyes with me and slapped her hands to her cheeks. "Oh my gosh, Chase! You have the most amazing tan I've ever seen!" she exclaimed, before dropping them into her lap again. "There. Is that better?" she added in a totally normal voice.

I laughed loud. "Much better. Thank you."

She shook her head. "You're such a nerd."

"But you love me!" I said, reaching to grab her knee playfully.

"I do." She smiled, covering my hand with hers and

squeezing. "I like hearing you laugh. I've missed it."

Her comment gave me pause, and I couldn't recall feeling this content for several months. I was glad she'd ridden with me today.

I grasped her hand tighter before releasing it and retuning mine to the wheel. "Thanks for talking to me, Britt. It's really helped. I know you'll be spending a lot of time with the blind and dumb . . ." I laughed when she gave me a puzzled look, "I mean Matt . . . when we get to Tempe, but don't be a stranger, okay? I like having you around. I wish everyone was super chill like you."

She smiled. "I'm cool like that, and since we're living right next door to each other, I'm sure we'll still see each other plenty. I'll probably be over often to drag Tana off Brett. She may need constant reminding which house is hers."

"Or vice versa," I added with a chuckle.

"Don't get me wrong, I'm glad they're into each other, but there have been a few times I could've used some bleach for my eyes."

"So you don't care for public displays of affection?" I asked, knowing exactly what she was referring to, since I'd witnessed them together many times.

She shrugged. "Normally it doesn't bother me, but he's my brother . . . ick."

"Why don't you return the favor then? Make out with Matt in front of them."

"That's okay . . . really." She gave a half laugh as she pondered it over. "It would serve them right, but Matt definitely isn't the P.D.A. type."

"Totally reaffirms my opinion that he's a loser," I replied. "Why make your girl wait for some affection? Why make yourself wait? Stupid. Just do it. If people don't like it, they don't have to look."

"That's one thing I've always really liked about

you."

"What?" I asked, confused. "That I'll make out in public?"

"No, that you'll do whatever you want to do without caring what other people will think about it. It's a rare quality. So many of us allow ourselves to be dictated by fear of someone else's opinion."

I shrugged. "I think it's my life—I ought to be the one who lives it." She was wrong, though. I might do whatever I wanted, but it didn't mean I was completely fearless. There were lots of things that made me feel nervous or insecure. I tried not to let those things show or get in my way too often.

"Well, I agree, and I like it."

"Glad I have your approval."

"You do." She patted my arm briefly. "You're a good duck."

Ducks. Instantly, I was in Nikki's bathroom once again, watching her brush her teeth while I teased her about the rubber ducks in the tub.

I tried not to sigh. Everything reminded me of Nikki.

~Chapter Five~

Two days later, I glanced around my room with satisfaction, staring at Nikki's picture placed in its new home next to Turk. Other than a couple boxes of odds and ends, I was pretty much unpacked.

The apartment didn't resemble the typical bachelor pad, thanks to my mom giving me all her furniture since Greg's house was fully furnished. I doubted many college coeds could boast of massive overstuffed leather couches complete with a coffee table, end tables, lamps, rug and a matching entertainment center with big screen TV and state of the art surround sound. If it weren't for the fact the pictures on the walls consisted of sports or band posters stuck up with tacks and tape, it would've looked like we had a designer come in. Mom had set us up with our entire kitchen and dining supplies too.

I chuckled as I remembered her words.

"There will be no traditional college wooden spool tables or shelves made out of crates for my son."

"But mom," I'd replied with a grin. "That's half the fun, scavenging for useful things. You're robbing me of my college experience."

"Trust me, Chase. Scavenging sucks. Plus, you never know where those things have been. You can't possibly properly sterilize them, either. It's gross."

"True, but if we have a wild party, all this nice furniture could get ruined. If I have crappy stuff to start with, then it won't matter if it gets busted."

"Precisely, which is why you won't be having any

wild parties. This is part of your inheritance—I won't be buying you more later on. So unless you want destroyed furniture, I suggest you take care of it."

I laughed. "Is this your way of trying to ensure I behave while I'm gone?"

She snorted. "You, behave? Is that even a possibility?"

"Remember, I'm reformed now."

"You might be, but that doesn't mean the rest of the college is."

I hugged her tightly. "You know I'll take care of it because Dad bought most of it. As for the rest, I give no guarantees."

"I guess I'll have to settle for that," she grumbled, hugging me back. "But at least promise me you'll be careful. It's going to be hard for me without you around."

Things had grown serious then. "I'll miss you too . . . a lot."

I grabbed my keys off the dresser and left my apartment, almost bumping straight into Brittney as she left hers. She was dressed in a tiny, blue bikini top, cut off shorts, and flip-flops. I couldn't help letting my gaze wander over her fabulous figure.

"Wow! You're looking pretty good today." I chuckled. I wasn't used to seeing her quite this stripped down. "Where you headed?"

She smiled. "To my new job."

"Dressed like that?" I clasped my hands together. "Please tell me you got a job at Hooters! I swear I'll come eat there every day to support you."

"No." She laughed, shaking her head. "I'm working as a waitress for a restaurant called Poppy's Grill. He has a niece who has cancer. They're doing a fundraiser carwash today to help with medical expenses. I'm going there. You should bring your pickup, and get it washed."

"I'd be happy to," I replied, thinking of Nikki's dad who'd also died of cancer. It was a devastating disease. "Where's this place?"

She dug into her purse and pulled out a business card. "The address is on here. You and Brett should try the restaurant too. Tana and I ate there the other night when I applied. It's really good."

"Sounds awesome. I'll definitely come by after I'm done with weights this morning."

"Okay, see you later then." She started to walk away, and I stared after her.

"If you have a break maybe you can eat with me," I called out, spur of the moment.

She turned and grinned while walking backward. "If I'm not too wet and dirty, I'd like that." She continued on her way, and I stood there appreciating the view from the backside as well.

I'd always thought she was smokin' hot, but gradually she'd become more like a sister, especially as my relationship developed with Nikki. But seeing her like this today reminded me she wasn't my sister in any capacity. It kind of scared me to feel such a sharp flicker of interest. I thought that part of me had long been dead and buried.

Sighing, I rubbed a hand over my face. There was no way I could think of a relationship with Brittney. Besides the fact I was done with putting my heart through the ringer, she wasn't available, and even if she was, there was no way I was willing to risk our friendship. She was too important to me. If things went badly, I'd lose all of that.

My phone buzzed in my pocket and I pulled it out. Dude, where R U? the text from Brett read.

Leaving the house.

Ok. Wanted 2 make sure U were up. Tana

dropped me off here after breakfast with her mom & dad, so she has her car now. Britt is using mine 4 the day.

Figured as much. Just saw her leaving with it. On my way. See U in a few.

I pulled into the long line of waiting vehicles. Brett and I got out, handing the keys and a wad of cash to a soaking wet girl who was standing there with a clipboard.

"Looks like we'll be waiting here for a while," Brett said. "Shall we try the food?"

"Sure," I replied absently as I scanned the busy parking lot looking for Brittney. I found her working hard on a sleek new Mustang while some guy leaned against it ogling the view. I figured he was probably the owner of the car, but it still irritated me for some reason. "There's Britt." I gave Brett a nudge and nodded in her direction. "Let's go talk to her."

"Hey hottie," I said, grabbing her around the waist as she leaned over a bucket of soapy water. She squealed before I set her back on her feet.

"Chase!" She slapped me on the shoulder with her wet sponge, soaking my shirtsleeve. "You scared me to death!"

I laughed. "And now you got me all wet. I should dump this bucket over your head."

"Don't you dare!" She backed away. "Besides, it serves you right for scaring me like that."

"I won't." I grinned, noticing the guy was frowning at me. "Can you take a break, and come eat with us? Tana will be bringing her car any minute too."

"Yeah, they're rotating us in and out. I need to go check and see if it's okay if I do it now, though."

"Um, can someone finish washing my car at least? I paid good money for this," the man said, appearing irritated.

"Oh, I'd never leave without finishing, sir. Sorry," Brittney quickly spoke up.

I grabbed her sponge. "You go talk to your manager about lunch. I'll take care of it." I dipped it into the bucket, knelt down and started working. Brett grabbed another one and joined me.

"I'd rather the girl take care of it," the guy said in a huffy tone as Brittney walked away.

"And I'd rather you quit ogling my girlfriend like she's a piece of meat," I responded without looking up from my task. Brett cast a surprised glance in my direction.

The guy cleared his throat uncomfortably, but didn't say another word as Brett and I finished soaping and rinsing the remaining bumper section Brittney hadn't done yet.

"There you go!" Brett said as we stepped away. "Looks like my sister did a good job on the rest."

The man glanced between us, grumbling something under his breath before getting in his car and driving away.

"Pervert," Brett muttered.

"He's old enough to be her dad. He was only here looking for some action."

"Well, at least they got his money, right?" Brett elbowed me, and we threw the sponges in the bucket.

"I can go eat right now," Brittney said as she returned. "But we'll need to sit on the outdoor pavilion, because I'm not dressed appropriately to be inside, and I'm too dirty."

"Sounds hot," I said as I glanced toward the building. Summers here in the Valley of the Sun were blistering.

"It's not too bad. They have misters to help keep things cool." She led the way to the country themed patio. Several antique-bronzed metal tables and chairs sat under a ceiling of spaced, dark-stained wooden beams. Vines had grown from strategically placed pots, creeping around the posts and through the roof overhead, creating a nice canopy of filtered shade. Britt gestured toward a table for us. "This okay?"

"Looks good to me," I said, holding a chair for her before sitting between her and Brett.

"So have things been this busy all day?" Brett asked, staring at the long line of cars backed out of the parking lot and down the side of the street.

"Yeah, it's been incredible. It's great to see the outpouring of love for this little girl. I got to meet her yesterday. She's precious. I think they're going to bring her here later."

"How bad is she?" Brett asked.

Brittney shook her head and lowered her voice. "I don't think there's any hope, really. They're simply trying to make the best of the time they have with her."

The old anger at death began to raise its ugly head, crowding me with the helpless feeling I always dreaded. I'd seen it tear up the lives of too many people. I was sick of hearing about it happening to others. I was sick of it happening to me. I was happy when the waitress interrupted us to take our order.

"Hi, Brittney. What can I get you and your friends to drink?"

I flicked a glance up, pausing when I saw a stunning brunette. When she smiled, my gaze settled on her mouth, and I was captivated. There was something about her that reminded me of Nikki.

"Hey, Jennifer. This is my twin brother, Brett, and one of our best friends, Chase Walker."

"Pleasure to meet you both," she said as she handed us menus.

"Nice to meet you," I replied with a nod, dragging

my stare from her lips to her eyes with some effort.

"Oh, and you remember my friend, Tana, from the other night," Brittney added as Tana approached the table with a wave.

"I do. Hi, again."

Tana smiled and seated herself next to Brett. Pushing her black hair behind her ear, she leaned to give him a quick kiss on the cheek. "Sorry I'm late. It took forever to find a parking spot."

"No worries. We were just getting started."

Their voices faded away into the background while I studied Jennifer, trying to figure out exactly what it was that reminded me of Nikki. She was about the same height and body type, maybe somewhat taller, but her eyes were green. Her brown hair was pulled into a ponytail, but looked like it might be around the same length—it was definitely the same shade. Her face was slightly rounder—she smiled at me again holding her pen poised. There it was—something about that smile, the way her plump lips curved, the corners angling upward as if she smiled a lot.

"Chase?" Brittney nudged me, and I looked at her.

"What?"

"Jennifer asked you what you want to drink."

"Oh, sorry. The heat is getting to me I guess," I lied.

Jennifer laughed, and it was a nice sound. "Let me help you with that."

I lifted an eyebrow, and she laughed again.

"Your drink?"

"Right. I'll take water, as cold as you've got it."

"Done. I'll be back in a minute to get your food order."

I watched her walk away, trying to imagine she was Nikki.

Brett's laughter drew my attention. "Is that the rise of the old female predator I see going on there?"

"What do you mean?" I asked.

"I mean you're staring at that girl like she's candy. I haven't seen that part of you in a long time."

"Actually, something about her reminds me of Nikki."

"Really?"

Everyone turned to stare.

"I don't see it," Brittney said.

"I do," Tana added. "Something about the way she smiles, and she has the same coloring."

"Exactly." I gave a sigh and leaned back in my chair, happy to know my mind wasn't playing tricks on me.

Brett squeezed my shoulder. "Keep your chin up, bro. Things will get better eventually."

Nodding, I picked up my menu and began reading. I didn't know if it would ever be possible.

~Chapter Six~

Another week went by, and things were starting to fall into a regular schedule for me. Basically, my life consisted of a lot of weight training and football practice, followed by weekends at home to help my mom with wedding preparations. If I ever had down time, I was either sleeping, playing video games, or surfing the internet—like I was tonight. I was turning into a boring old lady.

"Hey, man," Brett said, sticking his head in my doorway. "Brittney and Tana are here. They want to know if we'd like to go get some dinner with them tonight."

"Um, sure. Let me grab a hat and get my shoes on. I thought Brittney was going on a date with Matt tonight."

Brett shrugged. "He called and cancelled. I guess he had to work late. He rescheduled for tomorrow."

I shook my head as I walked to my closet. "The guy's an idiot. He better be straight up with her. I'll pound his face if he's messing around."

"I'll be right there beside you. She is *my* sister after all."

"Well, she feels like mine too. I don't want her getting hurt."

Brett stared for moment before clapping his hand on my back. "You're a good guy, Chase. Thanks for watching out for her."

"Any time. She's important to me. We had a good visit on the way down here, and I enjoyed spending some one-on-one time with her."

"Did you now?" Brett asked, and I noticed the mischievous twinkle in his eyes before he turned and walked through the door.

"Oh, come on, man. You know what I mean. It's not like that between Britt and me. She's one of the guys."

"Don't let her hear you call her that. She might punch you." He laughed.

"I meant it as a compliment. I like that I can hang and chill with her and not have it be weird."

"Not have what be weird?" Tana asked as we walked into the living room.

Damn. I forgot the girls were here. "Nothing. I was telling Brett how fun it is to be with the two of you and not have it feel strange." I gave her a hug and then Brittney.

"Why would it be like that?" She wasn't letting it go.

"No reason. How's your apartment looking? Did you finally get everything decorated like you wanted? I know you've both been shopping a lot lately." Girls were pickier about how they designed things. Our apartment had been done within two days. They'd been rearranging and fixing things since we moved in. Everything had to be exactly right.

"We did. You want to see it really quick before we go?" Brittney answered.

"Sure," I said with a shrug. "There's no rush."

She hooked her arm in mine, and Brett draped his around Tana as they led us next door. Their apartment was the exact mirror replica of ours, only it looked like a Better Homes and Gardens magazine exploded in the place. I'd helped my mom with enough staging in the homes she was selling to know this design style was considered shabby chic. It was done in whites, soft pinks and blues, with distressed wood pieces. It actually felt very homey.

"Wow. This is great," I said, really meaning it. "Martha Stewart would be proud."

Brett punched me. "Dude, you sound like a girl. You're gonna get killed in football if you talk like that."

I laughed and rubbed my shoulder. "What have I told you about punching my throwing arm? Besides, it's not my fault my mom talks about home décor all the time."

"It's the fact you actually listen I'm worried about." He gave me a suspicious looking glance.

"I think it's sweet," Brittney said coming to my defense, squeezing my arm. "Don't listen to him, Chase."

"See, she gets it."

"Come see my room, and tell me what you think of it." She started dragging me down the hall.

"And it's getting me into her room," I replied as we left. "Where did your knowledge get you?"

"I don't need knowledge to get me into Tana's room." He grinned.

Tana slapped his chest, and Brittney and I laughed.

"Doesn't look like you'll be in there any time soon, bro."

Brittney opened the door and pulled me into her space. I didn't really notice the rest of her room, because the pictures on her wall caught my attention immediately. She'd enlarged some of her cheerleading pictures and had them mounted. There were three oversized ones of her, and mingled into the rest of the collage were multiple ones of her high school squad with several larger pictures of her, Tana, and Nikki laughing and posing together. They were pictures I'd never seen before.

I gravitated toward them, wanting to study them closer. Involuntarily my hand reached to stroke Nikki's face.

"These are beautiful," I said softly.

"I thought you might like them. She was so happy."

"You all look wonderful. I've never seen these."

"My mom came and took them. She did this as a graduation surprise. I'd forgotten about her taking them. Nikki never saw them either."

"What game were these taken at?"

Her face fell slightly. "At the homecoming game."

My heart clenched tightly, memories of that night—both good and bad—washing over me. "So these are some of the last pictures taken of her, other than the ones she and I took at the dance together. You need to tell your mom to give these to Justine. She would really like to have them. Nikki's . . ." I couldn't bring myself to say the word, "being gone, has been hard on her."

"I know. I've been to visit her a couple times—not nearly as much as you have, though. It's nice you stay in touch with them as often as you do"

I shrugged. "They're a part of my family. She and my mom are best friends, and Timmy and Clara need me now that Nikki's gone."

"You're their connection to her," she said, patting my arm.

"They'd be better off with her instead. I wish I could give her back to them." My eyes were still glued to her face.

"This wasn't your fault, Chase. You don't need to try to repay something you don't owe."

The panic welled inside me. "It was my fault, Britt. She was breaking the rules, sneaking out to meet me. If I hadn't encouraged her to do that, her accident would've never happened."

She grabbed my chin and turned my face toward hers. I stared into her big blue eyes. "Did you ask her to sleep with you?"

"I told her I wanted to." I swallowed thickly.

"Answer the question, Chase. Did you ask her to sleep with you?"

I slowly shook my head. "No. She surprised me with it."

"Did you set up the place and time to meet?"

Again I shook my head. "No. She wanted it to be special. She suggested when and where."

"This was *her* choice, not yours. She made the plans. You're not at fault here—not in any way. Why can't you see that?" She released my chin and brushed her hand gently along my cheek.

"Because if she'd never met me, then it wouldn't have been an issue."

"If she'd never met you, it could've been some other guy she was with. You can't play the "what if" game. Things happen every day—sometimes horrible things—we are powerless to change. Stop trying to take the blame for what happened. Stop trying to make up for it, and just be yourself. Live your life and be happy."

"I don't know how." It was the most honest thing I could say.

She nodded. "I can understand that. We're all a little scarred from it." She paused and observed the pictures again. "I guess we need to concentrate on remembering the good things, and do our best to stick together and work through one day at a time. You've grieved for nine months now. I know it's harder for you, because you loved her in a different capacity than the rest of us, but we really do want to help you."

"I know—and I appreciate it."

She hugged me briefly before heading toward the door. "Come on. Let's go get some dinner."

I cast one more longing glance at her wall before I followed.

~Chapter Seven~

Brett and Tana wanted to go to The Devil's Pit. It was a swanky sports grill and bar on Mill Avenue rumored to be a favorite place among the ASU Sun Devil crowd. It didn't appear to be too busy when we pulled up, since school hadn't started yet, but right away I noticed a potential problem.

"Hey, isn't that Matt's car?" I asked Brett discretely when we got out, and he glanced in the direction I nodded.

"Sure looks like it." His brows furrowed as we followed the girls inside.

A hostess greeted us at the door and ushered us to a booth in the corner, but not before I caught a glimpse of Matt sitting next to a girl in the bar area. I cast Brittney a glance and then Brett to see if either of them had noticed. Brett had, but he shook his head, gesturing for me to be quiet. I knew he didn't want to ruin Brittney's night, but I wanted to beat the guy and find out what the heck he was doing. Britt was a great girl, and she didn't deserve to be treated this way.

Tana slid into the booth first, then Brett. Brittney moved in on the other side and scooted around by Tana, leaving me a place to sit beside her.

We ordered drinks and began looking through the menu. I kept getting distracted by the sports news on one of the many flat screen televisions around the ceiling of the neon-lit restaurant, but I couldn't help glancing occasionally toward the bar. I didn't know if I was hoping Brittney would see Matt, or not. I definitely didn't want her to get hurt, but if he was the cheating idiot I thought he was, then I'd be happy if he got caught, for sure. He may have managed to get a spot on the team too, but I hadn't liked him since I'd first moved to Silver Creek. I never could figure out how he and Britt had gotten together in the first place.

"What are you getting?" Brittney asked, nudging my elbow.

I returned my gaze to the menu. "Hmm . . . I'm not sure. The Devil Burger sounds good, and it's their signature dish, so I might try that."

"It does look good." Her eyes flicked over the page. "They have southwestern chicken wraps. I might try those. Ugh, there are too many good choices. I always get something and then wish I had something different."

I chuckled. "Everyone else's plate looks better than the one you have?"

"Exactly. Then I'm bummed because I wasted my money."

"Tell you what—you order your chicken wrap, I'll order the burger, and we can share with each other. I'll give you half of mine, if you give me half of yours."

Her eyes widened and she grinned. "You'd do that for me? Really?"

"Of course I would. I can't let you go home feeling bummed, can I? What kind of friend would I be?"

"You could never be a bad friend, Chase. I don't think it's in your chemical makeup."

I wrapped my arm around her shoulders and gave her a brief squeeze. "I'm glad you think so. You wouldn't have thought that if you'd known me a couple of years ago."

She looked like she wanted to ask me something, but the waitress brought our drinks, interrupting us. I rested my arm on the seat behind her, slouching as she took our orders. When she left, I leaned my head against the booth too.

"Are you tired?" Brett asked.

"Exhausted. Aren't you? We worked out hard today. I feel like I could sleep for a year."

"We should've let you guys stay home," Tana spoke up. "Especially since you have football practice again tomorrow. You need your rest."

"We'll be okay," Bret said. "This is nice, and we needed to eat anyway."

"And there's no dishes this way," I added.

"Please. You both know you wouldn't have cooked. Brett would've ordered a pizza if we hadn't invited you." Brittney smiled. "He hates to cook."

"You're right." Brett grinned. "I see a lot of pizza in our future."

"Well, we didn't have any groceries to cook with anyway. We still need to go shopping tonight and get some," I reminded.

"Maybe we can all go after dinner then," Tana suggested. "Britt and I need some more too."

"Sounds like a plan. Let's do it." I glanced between the twins who both nodded in agreement.

Brittney suddenly stiffened, and I turned to follow her gaze, seeing Matt walk from the bar with his arm draped around the curvy brunette. They were laughing boisterously over something, and his hand slid down to pinch her on the rear.

"Well, now I know what he was working on," Brittney whispered as she watched him walk through the front door.

"Say the word, Britt, and I'll go out there and pound his ass." I was pissed for her. Any guy would have to be blind not to see what a catch she was.

"I'm right there with him," Brett added as the four of us watched through the window. The two of them were kissing on the sidewalk as they moved toward Matt's car. We watched them until they were out of view. I ground my teeth together—so much for no public displays of affection. Had he raised his head up for two seconds he'd have seen us gawking at them.

"No. Leave him," she said, and I stared at her.

"Don't let him treat you this way, Brittney. He doesn't deserve you."

"I'm not letting him treat me this way," she said, lifting her chin a notch. "We're through. He just doesn't know it yet."

"Please say you're gonna let me be the one to tell him. I'd really love to punch the guy right now."

She smiled a bit dejectedly, and patted me gently on the leg. "Thanks, but no. He's supposed to pick me up for breakfast tomorrow. I'll tell him when he comes."

"I'm sorry, Brittney," Tana said, hugging her best friend. "Are you okay?"

She nodded, and grabbed her purse. "I will be, but I don't feel much like eating right now. I think I'll call a cab and go home, if you don't mind." She threw some money on the table. "That should cover my dinner."

"Wait," I said, grabbing my wallet and throwing some bills down too. "Brett, there's enough for my meal and some extra to help with groceries. If you and Tana will take care of that, I'll make sure Brittney gets home okay. I'm beat tonight. Have them box my food, and I'll eat it tomorrow. I can hardly stay awake."

"We can come now too. Are you sure?" Tana asked glancing between Brittney and me.

"No, eat your dinner. I'm sorry I ruined everyone's plans," Brittney said.

"You didn't," I replied, squeezing her shoulders briefly. "I'm going to get the hostess to call us a cab."

I left her with Brett and Tana while I walked to the hostess station for help. I saw Matt leaning against his car with the girl pinned beneath him as he kissed her. He obviously didn't care about who saw him. Did he think he was going to get away with it?

My hands clenched into fists, and I wished I could go yank him back by his sandy brown hair and beat his face. He stayed there long enough I worried he'd be there when our cab showed up. How would I get Brittney to the car without causing a big scene? I cast a worried glance in her direction. She was still talking to Brett and Tana. I was glad—she didn't need to see this. Finally, Matt helped the girl into the car and quickly joined her before they drove away. Not five seconds passed before our cab pulled up.

"Brittney," I called, signaling to her, and she joined me. I ushered her outside and opened the door, sliding in behind her.

"Desert Breeze Apartments near Southern and Rural Road, please," I leaned forward and told the driver then settled into my seat. I closed my eyes and sighed deeply.

"You really are tired, aren't you?" she asked after a couple of minutes. "You weren't saying that as an excuse to come with me."

"I'm beat," I said with a soft chuckle. "They've been running us hard." I gave her a heavily lidded stare and grinned. "Don't think I'm a wimp now, okay?"

"Whatever. I'd be surprised if you weren't tired. You helped us carry in all those boxes, bags, and furniture items we bought today too."

"Brett seems to be fine."

"He didn't carry half of what you did. Plus, he stopped and made out with Tana every time he brought something in."

"Disgusting," I said with a scrunched up face.

"Pitiful, indeed," she added, and we both laughed, the golden glow of the streetlights brushing back and forth across us. I watched her for a few moments as the driver sped down the road, weaving through the evening traffic.

"Aren't we a couple of sourpuss losers?"

"Yeah, but better a loser than having to be the one making out with Brett or Tana if you ask me."

"Here, here," I replied, enjoying our banter at the expense of our friends. "That would be wrong for both of us on so many levels." I pretended to shudder, and she laughed harder.

The cab stopped outside our complex, I paid the driver and we got out.

"Here's some money for my share of the cab," she said, handing me a few dollars.

"Don't worry about it. It'll be my treat. It was totally worth the chance to hit my pillow earlier than expected."

She smiled, but didn't argue as we walked up the stairs together. "Do you have your key?" she asked.

"Yes, I do," I replied, dangling them to show her.

"Okay, good. I guess I'll see you tomorrow then."

"Sounds like a plan. Get some rest."

She gave me a quick embrace, and both of us entered our apartments. I went straight to my room and sat down long enough to remove my shoes and hat before flopping onto my pillow. I stared at Nikki's picture for a minute in the dim light and slowly let my eyes drift shut to her image.

The air conditioning unit clicked off, and the house got really quiet. I could hear something strange, though, and I strained my ears trying to figure it out. I listen for several minutes to the random sounds before I finally realized what it was. Brittney's bedroom shared a wall with mine. She was crying in her room—sobbing from the sounds of it.

I groaned and rubbed my forehead. Damn that

Matt. How could he do this to her? I was glad she was dumping him, yes, but I didn't want to see her hurting either. I knew what it was like to lay in bed and ache for the person you wanted to be with.

Without considering anything, I got out of bed and went next door. I tried the knob and it was open, so I walked in. I was going to have to talk to her about that. We didn't live in the country anymore. I went to her room and knocked.

"You decent, Britt?"

"Yeah," came the hiccupped reply.

I stepped inside. The light was off, but I could see her form curled up in the corner of the bed under the far wall's window.

"I could hear you crying," I explained, not knowing what else to say.

"Sorry." She didn't move.

I went over and crawled next to her, leaning against the headboard. "Come here."

She snuggled into my arms immediately, still crying, and I stroked her hair, trying to soothe her somehow. My eyelids grew heavier with each passing minute, and I tried to fight the exhaustion, but I couldn't hold it back. I decided to rest my eyes for a few seconds.

~Chapter Eight~

Nikki and I were in the meadow by the creek sitting against a tree. She was wrapped in my arms, and it felt good to have her there.

"I've missed you," I said, kissing her brown hair softly as I stroked my hand over her short white sundress. We were both barefoot, and I was wearing a white button-up shirt that hung open along with a pair of kaki colored pants rolled at the cuff. I couldn't remember where I'd gotten them—they weren't my normal style.

She tilted her head so she could stare at me, her brown eyes sparkling brightly. "I've missed you too." Her voice was like music to my ears, a sound I could get lost in over and over again.

"Say something else to me," I ordered and she laughed.

"Like what?"

I sighed. "That was perfect. Don't stop talking or laughing. I love the sound of your voice." I squeezed her tighter, trying to get closer.

"I enjoy yours too." She slid her fingers up, tracing my lips, and I kissed them, my heart feeling like it was overflowing with joy. I'd never been as content as I was in this moment.

"You seem happy, but your eyes look sad and guarded." Her fingers moved their way to my brow. "Why?"

I stilled, wondering why she would see that. "Probably because you left me. I've been searching for you frantically. I never thought I'd see you again."

She nodded, and the sparkle in her own eyes dimmed. "I know. What happened to us wasn't very fair, was it?" She turned away slightly focusing in the direction of the creek. "Torn apart as our lives were barely beginning. I'm sorry it had to be that way."

"*Why* did it have to be that way?"

She shrugged. "I don't know. It just did."

"Well, I don't like it. It's been horrible without you."

"I know, and I'm sorry." She scooted up, brushing her lips across mine, and I slid my hand behind her neck in an attempt to keep her there and kiss her deeper. She smiled against my mouth and relented, allowing me the access I desperately sought.

My tongue slipped inside, touching hers, and the same old sparks exploded within me. I groaned as she moved, straddling my lap, so she was slightly above me now. Her hair fell in a dark curtain, surrounding both our faces in a little cocoon all to ourselves. It was longer than I remembered it, and I loved it.

I slid both my hands up the sides of her face, holding her lovely cheeks while the tips of my fingers tangled near the roots of her glorious locks. She tasted incredibly sweet, and I knew she was a treat I'd never get my fill of.

Releasing her, I trailed my fingers to her waist, rolling her over and pinning her on the ground beneath me. She laughed as I kissed my way down her neck, and I could feel her fingertips dancing down the skin of my back, underneath my unbuttoned shirt. It felt wonderful to have her touch me that way again.

"Why'd you wait so long to come to me?" I whispered against her skin, unable to pull my lips away.

"I've always been with you, Chase. You were too caught up in your own grief to notice I never left."

I lifted my head, pausing so I could search her eyes.

"My heart has been breaking. There were days I didn't know if I'd be able to go on."

She had a sad expression. "I know it's been difficult, but you're healing better now. That's good to see."

"I'm only healing because you're here with me again. I'm never going to let you go."

She didn't speak, but the glimmer in her eyes dimmed.

"What is it?" I asked, feeling apprehensive.

"I can't stay. I only came so you would know you're on the right track."

"I don't know what you mean."

She didn't speak for a moment, but when she did, her fingers traced over my heart. "Stop looking at your past and the things you can't change. They're done and over with." She brushed the side of my cheek. "Now is the time for you to look to the future, grasp it by the hand . . . ,"

". . . And decide where you want to go," I finished for her. "I've read the letter you left me in your journal so many times I have that part memorized. What future, Nikki? I'm doing my best to try and understand, but I'm just going through the motions." I stared, memorizing the planes of her beautiful face, not wanting to blink for fear she'd disappear.

"Chase?" Another voice intruded on us, calling from a distance, and I sat up, not recognizing it at first. "Chase?"

I looked at Nikki and smiled. "It's Brittney. Come on. She'll be so happy to see you." I pulled her to her feet and started running in the direction of Brittney's voice. I saw her standing in the middle of the field between the creek and the ranch house, her light-yellow dress blowing in the breeze around her. "Over here, Britt!" I called excitedly. "Look who's here!"

I turned, realizing Nikki's hand had slipped from

mine, and she was standing several feet behind me. She smiled softly, but there was a tear running down her cheek. "What's the matter, Nikki? Don't you want to see her?"

"This is as far as I can go," she said, staying where she was.

"What do you mean?" I glanced toward Brittney then back to her, feeling confused.

"Go to her. It's okay." Another tear fell, racing down her face, but she smiled wider.

"I can't. You're crying. I need to stay with you." I hurried over and grabbed her hand.

She shook her head. "I love you more than anything. You'll always be with me wherever I go, because I hold you in my heart. You're a piece of my very soul." She started to fade away.

"Don't leave me, Nikki. Stay here, please. I've tried really hard, but I can't do this on my own." I tried to hang on, attempting to grip her tighter.

"You don't have to, Chase. You're not alone." Her voice grew softer, carrying away on the breeze, so I had to strain to hear. "Go to her," she whispered. "I love you. Go."

"Nikki! Nikki!" I bolted awake calling her name, searching the room frantically.

"Chase? It's okay. You were dreaming. Chase?" Brittney's placed her hand against my heaving chest. The sheets of her bed were tangled around us, and the morning light was coming in through the window.

"What am I doing here?" I was totally confused, staring at the images on Brittney's wall.

"You heard me crying last night, and you came to comfort me. Remember? I think we both fell asleep. You were really tired." Her stare was wide and full of concern.

"I remember." I closed my eyes for a second, Nikki's

image still burning inside them. I felt Brittney's hand stroking my stomach in a comforting gesture, immediately causing a not-so-comforting reaction. "I've gotta go." I hastily threw the covers off, jumped up and hurried to the door, throwing it open as I headed down the hall.

"Chase," Brittney's voice called after me as I stepped out the front door, and I paused, afraid to look at her. I closed my eyes when I felt her hands slide over my shoulders. "Are you all right? You were calling for Nikki. You sounded panicked."

"I . . . I . . . " I couldn't talk about it, not with Brittney. I wasn't ready. "I can't do this right now." I stepped away.

"Chase, will you look at me?"

I clenched my teeth and took a breath, steeling myself as I turned. Her blonde hair was slightly tousled, and she had mascara smeared beneath her big blue eyes. She was beautiful, and I wanted to scream. When had I started noticing her this way? She was one of my best friends, nothing more.

"I wanted to thank you for taking care of me last night. It meant a lot. I'm not sure what happened in there this morning, but if you ever need to talk, please know I'm here for you." She stood on her tiptoes and wrapped her arms around my neck.

I slipped my arms around her loosely, not wanting to return the embrace—but wanting to at the same time. I sighed heavily as I laid my cheek against her hair. It smelled good, but not the same scent as Nikki's.

"Are we okay? You seem different." She pulled away so she could look at me, and I stared into her questioning eyes, not knowing how to answer.

"What the hell is going on here?"

We both turned to find Matt standing there, an angry scowl across his features.

This day was going from bad to worse, I could quickly see. I pushed Brittney behind me.

"I always knew you were after my girl, Walker!"

Brittney screamed as he threw his first punch, which I managed to dodge, but his second fist followed closely behind. I caught his hand and twisted it around behind him, grabbing him by the neck, shoving his face and chest against the plaster wall.

"If anyone deserves to be hit this morning it's you, you jackass," I whispered in his ear.

Brett appeared from our door rubbing his face, still dressed in his clothes from yesterday, followed by a bleary eyed Tana. "What's going on?" he asked.

"I found your sister and Chase together," Matt spat.

"No you didn't," Brittney quickly said. "You found me thanking Chase for his help. He heard me crying and came to check on me."

"She was crying because she saw you making out with some bimbo at The Devil's Pit last night," I added, twisting his arm higher. "Who needs to be punched now? Say the word, Britt."

"No. Let him go. I can deal with this."

I pushed away as I released him, feeling my emotions boiling to the surface.

Matt slowly turned around, rubbing his arm as he took in our angry faces before finally settling on Brittney's.

"Brittney, I . . ."

"Save it, Matt. Your actions spoke loud enough. We're through." She folded her arms as she stared at him.

"Just like that?" he asked incredulously.

"Just like that."

"We've been together for over two years now. I can't believe you'd throw it away because of one small indiscretion."

I wanted to pound his face, but I remained still.

"How do I know it's only been one? That's the thing—if it's been one, it could be more. It violated my trust in you, and now I can't believe anything you say. You could've been hooking up with people this whole time."

"So could you. We all know Walker's been desperate to get into your pants from the first day he saw you."

I immediately jumped forward. "You son-of-a . . ."

"Chase!" Brittney stepped between us, pushing me backward, and I was surprised how strong she was. "I've got this." She turned to face Matt. "Everyone here knows that's not true, Matt. Chase was always crazy about Nikki. He never made any kind of advances toward me. That's the difference between you and me—if he *had* shown interest, I would've broken up with you before I moved on to him. I'm not a cheater."

"Whatever. Just stay clear of me. All of you." He started walking toward the stairs.

"See you at practice, Matt." I couldn't help adding the goad. I'd be more than happy to take out my aggression on the field.

He paused for a moment, glancing back to glare at me, before he turned and headed down the steps out of site.

Tana wrapped her arms around Brittney. "Are you going to be okay, sweetie?" she crooned.

"Yeah," Brittney replied, glancing at me as a few tears ran down her cheeks.

"Good riddance, if you ask me," Brett grumbled.

"No one asked you," Tana snapped before steering Brittney toward the apartment they shared.

"Come on, Brett. Let the girls work it out together before we mess things up worse."

He nodded, and we walked inside our apartment.

I shook my head. "First two weeks here, and people are already in beds they don't belong in."

He laughed. "In my defense, Tana and I fell asleep together on the couch watching a movie. We were trying to be super quiet so we wouldn't wake you."

"Well, I wasn't here. I was asleep in your sister's bed."

"I'm not sure how I feel about that," he said, eyeing me.

"I'm not sure how I feel about it either, but if you're going to hit me, can you wait until I get up again? I'm going back to bed to see if I can start this day over." I pushed open my door and walked in.

"Chase?"

"Yeah?" I turned to find him standing inside.

"Do you like, Brittney? I mean in *that* way?"

My breath caught, and I suddenly felt like a ball of nerves about to explode. "I don't know how to answer your question right now."

He nodded and stayed there for a second staring.

"Was there something else?" I asked.

He sighed. "No, not really. I only wanted you to know I'm cool with it if you do decide you like her. She can't do any better than you. If I'm being honest . . . I've kinda been hoping something might eventually happen between you two." He moved into the hall, shutting the door behind him and left me staring at the spot where he'd stood a moment ago.

I took a step backward and sat heavily on my bed before leaning my elbows on my knees and thrusting my hands into my hair.

What the hell was happening?

~Chapter Nine~

It had been a week, and I didn't know how much longer I could manage to avoid her. I'd thrown myself into football practice with a vengeance. Matt never made any attempt to egg me on, other than to give me vicious looking stares. Part of the reason may have been there were strict no tolerance policies regarding fighting amongst team players. If we did it, we risked getting kicked off the team, but whatever, Matt wasn't my problem.

I'd gone home for the weekend and moped around, spending a good chunk of time sitting by Nikki's grave while I tried to decipher the crazy dream I'd had about her and Brittney. I didn't dream of her often, and when I did, it was usually some sort of nightmare involving her car accident. But even those dreams had faded after a few months. I'd never had a dream like this before.

While I wasn't sure I believed in messages from beyond the grave, this dream had certainly seemed to carry one. It had opened my eyes to something I'd refused to acknowledge . . . something I was still having difficulty acknowledging.

It wasn't possible for me to have feelings for Brittney. My heart wasn't in my chest anymore. It was buried in a grave next to the girl I loved, and I didn't need anyone else in my life. I'd had my chance at real love and was content to live with the memory of it forever. The few months we'd been together had filled me with enough warmth to last a lifetime.

Sure, I felt like the sun would never shine again, but

knowing I'd held its heat for one brief moment made it worth it. I knew if I had the chance to live it all over again—knowing what the outcome would be and the pain I would suffer—I'd do it in a heartbeat. Only this time I'd make sure every single moment was counted and enjoyed to the fullest possible measure.

Brittney. Her face resurfaced in my mind for the millionth time. Images of the two of us in her bed flashed through as well. I tried to tell myself it didn't matter—tried to tell myself the strangeness I felt was simply the result of waking up in bed with her. Any red-blooded guy would've been turned on a little, not just me. She was Brittney . . . one of my best friends. I couldn't feel that way about her; I shouldn't feel that way about her.

My phone rang, and I picked it up out of the cup holder next to me. "Hello?"

"You almost home?" Brett's voice said.

"Yeah, coming in on Country Club now, about to get on the freeway. Why?"

"The girls and I are getting ready to head to dinner and thought we'd wait for you if you were close."

I hesitated. I was starving. "No thanks, man. Go without me. I'm beat. I've been helping my mom set up her things at Greg's this weekend, and Grandpa had me weed the vegetable garden for Grandma. I think I'll go straight to bed, so I won't be tired for practice tomorrow."

"It's like five P.M., bro. You're turning into a grandma yourself if you're going to bed this early. Come eat with us."

I laughed, nestling the phone against my shoulder as I quickly checked my side mirror and switched lanes. "Grandma or not, I can still kick your butt any day of the week."

"That may be true, but even old ladies need to eat."

"I'm okay. I'll grab a sandwich before bed if I need to. Have fun. Tell the girls hi," I added hoping not to seem standoffish.

"Will do. Catch you later."

I sighed as I tossed the phone back into the cup holder, feeling like the biggest jerk in the world. I knew I needed to stop moping around at some point and face things in my life, but I didn't feel ready to take that leap yet.

I wasn't stupid. I knew Nikki was never coming back, no matter how much I hoped and wished for it. No matter how much I loved her and wanted her, we were done—through. Fate made the choice for us, and there was nothing I could do about it. I knew I needed to move forward, but I didn't want to. I'd been happy where I was—well, sort of.

My thoughts continued to eat at me as I drove my truck down the now-familiar route to my apartment. I parked in the numbered space reserved for my vehicle and grabbed my duffle bag from the passenger seat before I hopped out.

I slowly made my way up the stairs, pausing on the top step of the second floor landing when I saw Brittney sitting on my doorstep. She was staring at me, and I couldn't read the expression on her face.

"Hey, Britt. How are you?" I asked, my mouth going dry. Even dressed casually in shorts and a t-shirt with her hair pulled back, she was still extremely pretty.

She stood without speaking and opened the door to my apartment, going inside. I followed after—so much for avoiding her. She didn't look too happy. Instantly I worried maybe something had happened with Matt while I was gone.

"Is everything okay?" I asked, tossing my stuff on the floor when she flopped down onto the couch. I sat in the chair to her left—distance was a good thing. "Brett called and said you were all going to dinner. What happened?"

She sighed as she toyed with the frayed edge of her cutoff shorts. "I asked them to leave me behind when they said you weren't coming. I'm tired of being the third wheel tagging along with them all the time. Things aren't as fun when you aren't there."

I hadn't considered that when I'd been ditching her. I hadn't meant to make her uncomfortable.

She looked up, her expression hurt. "Why are you avoiding me?"

I didn't know what to say.

"I've gone over things in my head a billion times, trying to figure out how I might have offended you, and I can't think of anything," she continued. "Something is different, and it has been ever since you spent the night with me. I mean, I understand if the whole argument with Matt put you off, and you don't want to be caught in the middle of it, but he hasn't tried to call me since then. Brett says there haven't been any issues at practice, so I'm not sure what else is going on. You took off this weekend without asking the rest of us if we wanted a ride home, and then you backed out of dinner as soon as you returned. There's no way you're *that* tired. You spent half of last week holed up in your room sleeping. You didn't do anything with us."

She stopped, clearly waiting for me to say something.

"Sorry, Britt. I've had some things I've been trying to work through. I didn't mean to upset you." I took my ball cap off and rubbed my head, knowing I was making a bigger mess of things.

"I told you that you could come talk to me about things. You seemed so much better, and then all of a sudden you're avoiding us again. Why can't you talk to me like before? I want to help. That's what friends do for each other."

I grunted in frustration, more of a feeble attempt to laugh really. "I know, and I appreciate it. This was just something I needed to try and figure out on my own."

"Did you?" she asked.

"Did I what?"

"Get it figured out?"

I stared, my gaze resting on her appealing mouth before I quickly looked down, only to find it settling on the rest of her perfectly curved form. "No, I didn't," I replied with a sigh as I slumped in the chair. I was clearly attracted to her. I'd been happy for one second when I'd seen her there, on the doorstep. This was extremely irritating. I couldn't feel this way. Her friendship was invaluable right now. I didn't want to mess it up by coming on to her. Hell, I wasn't sure if she liked me at all. Plus, I felt like I was cheating on Nikki in the worst way by entertaining these ideas in my head.

"Is there anything I can do to help?" She appeared truly concerned.

I gave a wry smile and chuckled mostly to myself. "Nope. I think you're . . . you're doing good just like you are." Sitting up quickly, I patted her on the knee in what I hoped was a reassuring gesture and got up, grabbing my bag off the floor. I went to my room, dropping it onto my bed and unzipped it. I began putting away the clean clothes my mom washed for me while I was home.

She stepped inside my door, taking a few steps toward me, and I tried, unsuccessfully, not to feel excited she was there. "If nothing is wrong, then why do you keep leaving when I'm around? Seriously, I'm starting to feel like you're mad at me or something."

"I'm not mad at you, Britt, okay? Let's leave it at that." I yanked a shirt over the hanger in my hand and took it to my closet before repeating the action.

"You're acting like you are." She was biting her lip

in a worried gesture when I glanced at her.

"Well, I don't mean to." I reached into the bag for another shirt, pausing when I felt her hand on my arm.

"Please tell me what's wrong."

She was too close. I could smell the perfume she wore, and the soft scent called to me. I clenched my hands, balling them into fists as I closed my eyes, fighting the temptation.

"Chase?"

I lost the battle with that one word. I turned around, grabbed her face and kissed her, pressing my mouth hard and fast to hers before breaking away, stumbling a step backward.

She looked at me in shock, her trembling hand moving to brush against her lips.

"Go ahead. Yell at me. Tell me what a jerk I am for stealing a kiss. I deserve it. I need to hear it." I glared, straightening my spine—ready for her attack.

She moved toward me, looking me straight in the eyes. "I can't." She slid her arms around my neck and popped up on her tiptoes to kiss me again.

I groaned as I relented, wrapping my arms around her. This couldn't happen now. I was too needy, and I craved the feeling she was giving me. I crushed her body to mine, as our mouths tangled together, heat and passion running furiously to the surface between us. I felt her fingers digging into my skin, my shirt bunching beneath them. I broke from our embrace and pulled it over my head dropping it to the floor before stepping into the circle of her arms again, loving the feel of her hands sliding up against my bare skin. I pushed her back, brushing my bag off the bed before the two of us toppled together onto the soft mattress.

The sensible side of my brain was screaming obscenities, trying to stop me, but I didn't want to. I hadn't been with a girl in well over a year. I was tired of waiting, of feeling alone. I'd waited for Nikki, and look where it had gotten me. I was going to lose myself for a while in the arms of Brittney.

I broke away from her mouth, trailing kisses down her neck, along with a few nips against her skin. My hand slid up under her shirt, feeling the smooth satin of her stomach as I feathered kisses against her collarbone. Pushing her shirt farther out of the way, I trailed my tongue down to her belly button, and she arched against me.

"Chase," she breathed. "Chase, wait."

I didn't want her to stop me. "Shhh. It'll be fine, Nikki . . ."

She stiffened, and I froze in horror as I realized what I'd said.

I punched the wall, and she gave a slight shriek as I got off the bed. I grabbed my shirt off the floor and threw it back on before grabbing the keys to my truck off the dresser.

"Where are you going?" she asked, propping up on her elbows.

"Out. I can't do this right now." I headed for the door.

"Chase wait!" she called.

I spun around. "You wanted to know what the problem is? Well, there it is. I'm attracted to you, but I'm still in love with her! What am I supposed to do with that?"

Her eyes were wide and round. "I . . . I don't know."

"Well, neither do I." I slammed the door on my way out. I left the apartment, and ran down to my truck, peeling out of the parking lot. I tried to calm my raging hormones as I drove—I was so turned on I could hardly see straight.

My tires squealed into the parking lot of the gym, and I jumped out and ran inside. I went to the first available punching bag and started hitting it as hard as I could, not caring who was there or watching. All the blind rage that needed venting spilled from me as I hammered away, slamming my fists into the bag. It swung about wildly as I pummeled it over and over. The skin on my knuckles split open, leaving blood smears behind, but I kept going, too pissed off to stop.

I hated myself for betraying both Nikki and Brittney with my actions. I didn't deserve either of them. Everything inside me was too dark, tainted with something that smothered the good it touched. People like me didn't deserve to be happy, which is why I lost everyone I cared about. Well, if I was going to lose Brittney, it would be because she was angry with me, not because she was dead. I was determined to never allow myself such close attachment to another person that losing them would destroy me this badly.

Sweat dripped down my face as I poured all my exertion into beating the swinging device as if my life depended on it. I couldn't stop. I didn't want to stop. I wanted to keep going until I couldn't feel anything. I needed to find that place of blissful numbness once again.

There was no way for me to tell how long I'd been there when strong arms wrapped around me, pulling me away from the bloody bag. "That's enough slugger. It's dead now. It's dead." Brett's voice said softly.

I dropped to the mat, breathing heavily. The area had cleared but several of my teammates stood around the edges of the room casting cautious glances at me. I wondered which of them had called Brett.

He settled down next to me. "Talk to me, Chase. What can I do for you, bro?"

I felt like I was going to start sobbing. "Get me some damn blunt," I croaked. "I can't take this shit anymore."

~Chapter Ten~

I was in bed with the covers over my head in an attempt to block the brightly shining sun. I didn't have practice this afternoon, and I was determined to stay inside as long as possible. There was no way I was going to risk running into Brittney, who'd managed to safely vacate my room before Brett returned home with me last night.

Brett had tried talking to me while he bandaged my cracked and swollen knuckles. I'd managed to conclude that Brittney was the one who'd called him. He'd deduced I'd gone to the gym, and it ticked me off further that everyone seemed to read me so well.

My phone buzzed on my nightstand, and I groaned, debating whether or not to check it, but curiosity finally got the better of me. I felt a brief shot of panic when Greg's number popped up. He rarely called me from his cell phone, preferring to join my mom's calls instead.

"Hello?" I answered, hoping she was all right.

"Hey, kiddo. How you holding up?"

I relaxed instantly at his easy demeanor. He wouldn't be so laid back if something was wrong.

"I'm doing okay, I guess. How are you and Mom?"

"Really?" he continued, ignoring my question. "Because I heard you beat a punching bag to a bloody pulp last night. I thought maybe I should call down and see how things were going."

I was going to kill Brett. "I'm fine. Just needed to blow off some steam is all. How're the wedding plans going? Everything still working out? It's not too long now."

"It's still too long if you ask me. I'm more than ready to be married to your mom. I hate watching her things move in here without her."

I smiled, even though I didn't want to. "I'm glad the two of you found each other. She seems really happy when she's with you."

"I'm glad you think so. I never thought I'd be this lucky again. I was prepared to live my life as an old unmarried bachelor."

There was a pregnant pause between us as his words sunk in.

"Is that really a bad thing?" I asked, needing to know. I'd never gone to Greg for advice—outside of some casual football talk—but suddenly, given his history and how he'd lost his fiancée, he seemed to be exactly the person I needed.

"Very bad. I shut down until I cut myself off from any possibility of finding love again. I didn't want to date or do anything remotely like it."

"But you found my mom."

"I know. She struck me differently, or maybe my heart was finally healed. I knew when we met I had to know her better. Everything else happened on its own. If it's right, it won't have to be forced. It'll develop naturally."

"Didn't you ever feel like you were cheating on your girlfriend?"

"Not by then, but I'm sure I would've had I tried dating early on. It's hard to get over losing someone you love like that. You have these intense emotions for the person and nowhere to direct them anymore. It was a very confusing time."

"It has been for me too." It was nice to connect with someone who finally understood exactly what I felt like. "What helped you through it?"

"Let me ask you a question instead."

"Okay."

"Do you love your dad?"

I snorted. "Of course I do. You know that."

"Then how about me? Do you have any good feeling toward me?"

"You know I do, Greg. Where are you going with this?"

"Does having feelings for me make those emotions you have for your dad any less real?"

"No."

"So what's stopping you from dating other people then, Chase? Falling for someone else doesn't mean you love Nikki any less. It only means you love someone else too. You have a big heart—I've seen it. There's room for lots of people."

I pondered this for a moment before replying. "I'm too scared. What if something happens to . . . a new person I might fall for?"

"What if you both live happily until your ninety? Who's to say what may or may not happen? None of us are going to get out of this life alive, unfortunately, so it's up to each of us to decide how we want to live. Are you going to spend the rest of your days letting fear dictate how you should act, or are you going to grasp life with both hands and live it how you want? You should know, more than anyone, how precious time is."

That was true. He was giving me a lot to think about. "Is there another reason you called?"

"Well, yeah. I wanted to officially ask you to be my best man at the wedding. Your mom said she didn't think you'd do it, but I'd really like to have you stand up there with me."

I was shocked. The last I'd heard, they weren't going to have any attendants. "Yeah, sure. I'd be honored."

I could almost see his grin through the phone as he gave a short chuckle and murmured something to someone in the background.

"Tell mom I said I love her."

"I'll do that. Take it easy, son."

I ended the call, spotting Nikki's photo beside my bed and picking it up.

I traced her smile with my fingers, thinking perhaps what Greg said was true. I was starting to have some feelings for Brittney, but my love for Nikki hadn't dimmed or changed at all, that I could see. My heart still ached for her the same way it always had.

Could I move on? I sighed. Was it fair for me to move on with another person, while I was still emotionally attached to someone else?

I allowed myself to remember the kiss Brittney and I had shared. It had been hot, fiery, and I'd felt it all the way down to my toes. Was it simply the fact I'd been so long without someone which caused me to feel this way? Or was it that Brittney and I were really that powerful together? True, she'd been attempting to bring things to a halt when I'd spoken Nikki's name, but there was no doubt she'd been as into it as I had. But she was hurting also, and maybe her reaction was only mirroring her own loneliness after her break up with Matt.

There was only one way to find out.

I threw the covers back and got up, hurrying to my bedroom door. "Brett?" I listened for a reply but there was no sound in the house. He must be next door. I went outside, lifting my hand to knock, but decided against it when I observed my bandaged knuckles. I turned the knob and opened it a crack. "Brett?" I called again.

"In the kitchen, dude. What's up?"

I popped my head inside. He was helping Tana

make sandwiches.

"Can I talk to you outside for a minute?"

"Sure." He wiped his hands on a towel and joined me, giving me an expectant look.

"First off, you're dead meat," I began. "Quit ganging people up on me."

He squinted, running a hand through his spiky white-blond hair. "I'm not gonna lie. I've been worried about you, man. You've been scaring me lately, and when you asked me to help you get some drugs last night, I knew you were going from bad to worse. Someone needed to intervene."

"So you called Greg?" I folded my arms and stared him down.

"Under the circumstances, I felt he might be exactly who you needed to talk to. I'm not sorry if I crossed a line. You need help, and you don't seem willing to share with any of us."

I turned away, walking to the balcony railing and leaning against it. "I'm not trying to shut you out. It's just that you're too close to the situation."

"What situation?"

I looked back at him. "The situation with Brittney."

"You like her . . . a lot." It was a statement not a question.

I sighed. "I do."

"Well, I've been wondering how long it would take you to fess up. I'd say that's half your battle right there."

"It feels so . . . wrong. How can it be okay to be attracted to her when I still feel tied to Nikki?"

"You're always gonna be tied to Nikki, dude. She was a huge part of your life. She was a huge part of Brittney's as well. I'd think if anyone was going to understand, it would be her."

"Is she home?"

"Yeah, she's in her room still. She hasn't been out

yet this morning."

"I should go talk to her then."

Brett nodded. "That would be good. She was feeling pretty down last night."

I headed toward the door.

"Chase?"

"Yeah?"

"Try not to hurt her, okay?"

I gripped the knob. "I'll do my best."

I didn't say anything to Tana as I passed the kitchen, but she gave me a sorrowful look. Stopping outside of Brittney's door, I rapped lightly.

"Who is it?" she answered.

"It's me," I replied.

There were several moments of silence. "Come in, Chase," she finally said.

I stepped inside, finding her sitting on the edge of her bed in a tank top and small shorts. Her hair was messed up, and her mascara was smudged like she may have been crying again. I thought she looked beautiful, and immediately my body reacted to her. I gritted my teeth, trying to push forward.

"Sorry, about last night." I didn't know what else to say.

Her gaze drifted downward, resting on my bandaged hands. "Don't be. This is weird for both of us. We both loved her."

I nodded, staying clear across the room, not trusting myself to be any closer. "I'm not sure where to take things from here," I began, trying to muddle through sharing my feelings. "I don't want things to be weird between us, because I really do value your friendship. I didn't mean to get so carried away." Damn, I wanted to kiss her again. "I'm not sure I'm explaining things right."

She held up a hand. "Stop right there, Chase. I

know what you're trying to say, and it's okay with me."

"Really?" I asked, surprised and relieved she'd readily agreed. I'd made up my mind to ask her on a real date and see how things would go.

"Really. I know you love Nikki. You've been lonely, and I was there when it got too much for you. I mean, don't get me wrong, I enjoyed kissing you, but we're both definitely on the damaged side here. I'd hate for a rebound relationship to completely destroy our friendship. Let's pretend like this never happened okay?"

Wait. My mind was scrambling to keep up. She thought I didn't want anything to do with her now? I was completely confused. My body was practically screaming to throw her on the bed and do wicked things.

"I don't think—"

"Don't worry about it, Chase," she cut me off before glancing at her clock. "I need to get ready. I have a date in an hour."

I was floored. Here I was trying to tell her I liked her, and she'd called me a rebound. Now she was seeing someone else? My head was spinning. Last night must not have meant anything to her at all. "Who are you going with?" I asked, the words leaving a sour taste in my mouth.

"Jeff Stinson. He's a waiter from the restaurant. A bunch of us are going boating at Saguaro Lake. Would you like to come?"

I shook my head. "No. I don't have a date. Thanks anyway, though." I felt like I was gonna be sick.

"Oh! Neither does Jennifer! You want to go with her? She was the waitress you met before."

I snorted—the waitress that reminded me of Nikki. This day kept getting better and better.

"Come with me. It'll be fun, and it'll give you a

chance to meet new people."

I didn't know about fun, but it would give me the opportunity to be around Brittney. Maybe I'd have another chance to talk with her and straighten things out. At the very least, I could evaluate my own feelings.

"Well, I did promise my grandpa I'd try to do something fun. He's been on me lately because I haven't kept my word."

"Then it's settled!" She hopped off her bed and bounced over, wrapping her arms around me, and laying her head on my chest. I couldn't help hugging her back, forcing myself to release her when she stepped away. "Everything's going to work out fine, Chase. Just wait and see. You might even meet some girl who will sweep you off your feet!"

I could only smile at her numbly. I didn't want to meet anyone else, and this time I didn't delude myself . . . it wasn't because of Nikki, it was because of Brittney. I wanted her.

~Chapter Eleven~

"Hey. How you doing? Good to see you again." I offered my hand to the smiling Jennifer as we stood on the boat dock. Like me, she looked a slightly nervous too. She wiped her palm against the sarong draped around her very shapely hips and hot pink bikini before taking mine.

"I'm great. How are you?"

"As well as can be expected—being thrown together with a virtual stranger at the last minute." I grinned so she'd know I was teasing.

"Yeah, well, I got lucky. At least the stranger was cute."

Oh, we were going to get along fine . . . if I could quit staring at her smile like I'd never seen one before. "Then I must be lucky too."

She glanced down and concern suddenly filled her eyes. "Oh my gosh! What happened to your knuckles?"

I followed her line of sight to the scabbed cracks by my fingers. I released her and moved my hand to the small of her back, ushering her toward the others who were loading supplies onto the speedboat. "It's nothing—just got a little overaggressive with a punching bag last night." I laughed it off. "Do you like water skiing?" I asked, trying to keep the conversation flowing. I felt way out of practice.

"Actually, I've never been."

"You live in Arizona, and you've never been water skiing?"

"Nope. I've been jet skiing, though. That was fun."

She shifted her canvas bag onto her shoulder and glanced at me. "I'm kind of a book nerd. I love to read." She opened her bag allowing me to look in and see two books there.

Paranormal books. Like Nikki.

"My girlfriend likes those types of books too."

Her expression fell. "You have a girlfriend?"

I sighed, realizing I'd blundered. "Well, no, not exactly. She died several months ago." It didn't matter how many times I said the words—I still hated them. I'd never get used to it.

Her eyes widened in surprise. "Oh my gosh! How terrible! I'm so sorry, I didn't realize. It must've been very difficult for you." She placed a hand on my arm and squeezed gently.

I glanced across the reflective water of the lake with the towering red canyon walls around it, set off by the rich blue sky above. "It wasn't easy, that's for sure. This is actually the first real date I've been on since it happened." *Shut up, Chase!* My mind reeled. *Who talks about their dead girlfriend on a date?*

There was an awkward pause, and I could see she was searching for the right thing to say.

"Chase!" Brittney's voice broke through the silence, and I felt relief wash through me as I gave a sidelong glance in her direction. "Let's go." She smiled and waved her arm, encouraging us to get on the boat.

I guided Jennifer to a vacant spot near Brittney and sat down in between them. Brittney looked perfect in her turquoise and purple bikini, her thick blonde hair cascaded in waves down her back, and I couldn't help remember what it felt like between my fingers. I wanted to reach out and touch it again, but instead I leaned against the seat, placing both my arms behind the girls.

"Are we ready?" Jeff called as he started the engine.

"Yes!" everyone except me chorused, and I glanced

around at the other three couples I'd met, trying to remember all their names. What an awkward situation.

Jeff steered away from the dock with ease, and soon we were flying over the water. Both Brittney's and Jennifer's hair blew around wildly, tickling my arms. My breath caught for a moment when I turned to look at Jennifer—a thick strand whipped across her face, obscuring some of her features, but still allowed me to see her fabulous smile. It was like I was staring at Nikki. My pulse sped up rapidly, and I clenched my hands into fists. I wanted her to be Nikki. It could've easily been this way for real. This was how it was supposed to be.

Jennifer tucked her hair behind her ear before placing a hand on my leg. "Are you okay? You look like you're going to be sick. Does the water make you nauseous?" she shouted over the roar of the boat.

I shook my head. "Nah, I'm fine. It's just really windy." I needed to chill out, and quit acting like a lovesick idiot.

She nodded and glanced at the water rushing by the edge of the boat. "I love the smell of the lake. It reminds me of going fishing with my grandpa when I was little."

"You like to fish?" I tried to imagine her holding a rod and casting it.

"Yeah. I don't know if I'm any good at it, but it's fun. I like to set my pole up and then sit and read while I wait. Nothing beats enjoying a good book out-of-doors. Of course, it's probably not as much fun at the lakes here in the valley. It's too hot."

"I hear you. Days like today, when it's one hundred and ten degrees, make me really miss living in the White Mountains."

"Have you always lived there?"

I shook my head. "No, I'm originally from here. I lived most of my life in Scottsdale. We only moved to Silver Creek after my dad died. We moved there during my junior year, but it grew on me I guess. It's home now. How about you?"

"I'm originally from Layton, Utah, but my dad got a job working for US Airways in Phoenix about five years ago, so we moved. I miss Utah, but I like it here too. I'm not a big fan of the summer heat, but the rest of the year is nice. Plus, my uncle lives in Mesa, too. He's the one who owns the restaurant we work at. Where do you work?"

"I don't right now. I used to work as a lifeguard in Scottsdale. Since then I worked on my Grandpa's farm. I'm here on a full-ride football scholarship to ASU with a housing waver. It pays for my rent and part of my utilities. I saved quite a bit from my previous jobs, and my dad matched that money before he died, so I'm living off that until football season is over. Then I'll scout around for a new job."

She smiled. "So you're saying if I start to drown in the lake today, you'll come rescue me?"

I grinned. "That's exactly what I'm saying. Gotta put my training to use somewhere."

"Suddenly I feel a whole lot safer. I'm a tiny bit nervous about skiing."

"Have you ever snow skied?" I asked.

She shook her head. "No. I was too chicken to try it after my older brother went on a class trip and broke his leg. He's super athletic, and I'm not. I figured I better not risk it."

I briefly admired her form. "You must be doing something to stay in shape. You look pretty good to me."

She smiled, her cheeks pinking slightly. "Thanks. I use my bike to get around most of the time. It's cheaper than paying for gas."

"Well, it's working for you. I totally understand about gas prices. They suck. You've probably saved a lot of money by doing that." We weren't really talking about anything particularly important, but she seemed easy to get along with.

"It's helps significantly, plus it's good for me." She paused, giving me a perusing glance. "So you play football. Tell me about that. I'm assuming you've been doing it a while."

"I've played contact football since I was four years old. My dad thought it would build character."

"Well, since you have a full-ride scholarship to ASU, you must be awesome. Those are hard to get."

I shrugged. "I'm okay, I guess."

"Don't let him fool you. He's the bombdiggity when it comes to football players," Brittney broke in. I hadn't been aware she was listening. "He was named State Player of the Year in his division. His stats are incredible. Trust me when I say he's the best of the best."

I laughed. "I've paid her to be my personal cheerleader. You can't believe a word she says."

"Whatever," Brittney replied, rolling her eyes. "He's trying to be modest. I promise you he will knock your socks off. I could watch him play all day long and never get tired of it." She grabbed my hand and squeezed it, staring into my eyes. "Admit it—you're the best."

"That remains to be seen. My coaches haven't named any positions yet, and as a freshman, there's a good chance I won't get the starter spot."

"Where do you play?" Jennifer asked.

"He's the quarterback," Brittney responded before I could open my mouth. "And mark my words . . . he'll be the starter."

"Wow. That's amazing," Jennifer said, sounding truly impressed.

I couldn't stop staring at Brittney. "I had no idea you were such a fan."

She smiled and gripped my hand harder. "I'm your biggest fan. Don't ever forget it."

Something inside me flipped around, and my pulse sped up. I liked hearing her talk like this. Now if I could only make her see how well we could work together. "I won't. I think you're pretty great too."

"Aw, we're having a BFF moment. How sweet!" She gave me a quick hug and turned around to talk to Jeff before I could respond. What I was feeling had nothing to do with being best friends.

"I knew you two were acquainted, but I didn't realize you were so close," Jennifer said as Jeff steered the boat into a small cove nestled into the rocky canyon.

"Her twin brother is my best buddy, and she was best friends with my girlfriend too. We've hung around together a lot. She's a great girl."

"I've really enjoyed getting to know her through work. She's very sweet."

"I would have to agree." *Plus she's a fabulous kisser,* I mentally added. I snuck a peek at her skimpily clad form once again, remembering how silky her skin had felt against me during those all-too-brief moments in my bed. I wondered if she'd ever be there again.

"So what are you going to major in?" Jennifer asked, redirecting my attention.

"Sports medicine, I think. Mostly, I'm doing the general education thing right now—getting the required stuff out of the way."

"Do you hope to continue playing football after college?"

"That's my dream—yes. I've wanted to play pro for as long as I can remember. Hopefully, I'll be good enough to make it there."

"I hope you can too. It would be awesome. Then I could say I knew you when." She laughed, and I smiled.

"Maybe. What are you studying?"

"Culinary Arts with a minor in small business management. I want my own restaurant someday."

"Really? I'm guessing you cook then."

She laughed. "When I'm not reading, I love to cook. Then I like to read while I'm eating what I made."

"So does this have anything to do with your uncle owning a restaurant?"

"Maybe. It does sort of run in the family. We have a lot of good cooks."

"What kind of place do you want to open?"

"Definitely an Italian place. I want to live abroad for a few months and go to a culinary school in Italy after I graduate here."

"So you want to be one of those fancy chefs then?"

She shook her head. "No. I want to perfect the home-grown taste. Things like you'd find in those cozy authentic bistro kinds of places. I want that homey old-world type of feel, full of warmth, laughter, and really good food." Her face was totally lit up as she described it, and I could picture exactly what she was talking about. It made me hungry.

"Well, I'm sold. Tell me when you open for business, and I'll be there."

She grinned widely and shoved me playfully. "Quit teasing. I know I sound crazy, but it does excite me."

"I'm not joking in the least," I replied. "You painted the picture well. I'd take you to the car right now if we could find a place like that to eat. I skipped breakfast." I glanced around. "Of course there's the minor problem of all this water. I'm not too big on swimming back to the marina."

"Good thing we brought lots of food then, huh?"

"A very good thing." I smiled and she returned it.

"I think I like you," she said. "You're fun. I'm glad. I wasn't too sure about coming today."

Jeff anchored the boat next to a small dock, which

ran into the cove, and I stood and offered my hand, helping her up onto the platform.

"I'm happy I made a good first impression. To be honest, I feel a bit out of my element when it comes to dating these days."

She linked her arm through mine. "Don't worry. You're doing fine."

I cast a glance at Jeff and Brittney setting up a picnic area, the two of them laughing together. I sighed. Today was bound to be interesting.

~Chapter Twelve~

The campfire crackled, and the smell of the roasted marshmallows and chocolate in the air was great. We were worn out from a fabulous day of water skiing, swimming, laughing, and generally having a great time.

I was trying really hard to concentrate on what Jennifer was saying while she made the s'mores, but my eyes kept drifting to where Jeff and Brittney lay together on a blanket. He was holding her in his arms and placing soft tender kisses on her face.

They liked each other. It was killing me.

I had to hand it to Brittney. She'd been true to her word when she said she was going to pretend like nothing had happened between us. I had no idea how she was in such control of her feelings. I was in complete turmoil inside, torn between wanting to kick the crap out of Jeff before dragging Brittney away, and actually paying attention to Jennifer because there was honestly something I liked about her too.

The other couples had wandered off to their own dark corners, leaving Jennifer and I together at the campfire making our dessert.

I had fun with her today, and enjoyed trying to teach her how to ski. She'd managed to get up on her skis occasionally, but spent most of her time being dragged behind the boat instead. The new joke was that she'd been paired with the ex-lifeguard for a reason.

She was a great sport, I thought, even when she lost her bikini top in the water. I fetched it while she attempted to keep herself covered and helped her get it back on. She'd been bright red with embarrassment. I hadn't minded one bit. She was a beautiful girl, and I enjoyed looking at her. If Brittney weren't in the picture, I'd already be planning when I could ask her out again.

"Here you go," she said, breaking into my musings. She held the gooey treat up to my mouth, and I took a bite, chewing slowly. "How is it?"

I closed my eyes and finished it, swallowing before I answered. "Pretty good. I can see why you're gonna be a chef."

She snorted. "I don't think s'mores qualify as cooking." She popped the rest into her mouth.

"Sure they do. You don't want to overcook the marshmallow, or leave the chocolate too hard. That's important."

"I didn't realize I was with a s'more connoisseur." She laughed as she licked her lips for stray marshmallow.

"I take my dessert very seriously," I replied with a deadpan expression, and she giggled. "Here, you missed a spot." I ran my finger under her lip where she had some smeared, holding it up for her to see.

She studied it briefly before wrapping her lips around my finger and licking it clean. I sat there, stunned, as I watched, and suddenly I was very turned on. She pulled away and stared at me, firelight caressing her features.

I was frozen as I stared, wondering what she'd do next.

She leaned in close, her gaze falling to my mouth. "I want to kiss you, Chase. Is that okay?" she whispered.

I held my breath for several seconds before I nodded.

She closed the distance between us, her lips gently touching mine, pressing there for a few moments before she pulled back, looking at me innocently.

Breathe, I reminded myself. *You've done this before.*

"Let's go for a walk," I said, standing to offer her my hand. She took it, and I steered her toward the dock.

"Where we going?" she asked.

"I thought we could enjoy the moonlight on the water better away from the fire."

"Sounds nice."

She sat down with me when we reached the end, both of us dangling our feet in the lake.

"It's really pretty out here," she said.

I nodded.

"I hope I didn't offend you a moment ago."

I was confused. "Offend me?"

"By asking you if I could kiss you." She smiled softly, and again I was struck by the resemblance to Nikki.

I glanced away. I wanted to like her for her, not because of a ghost tormenting my every waking moment. It wouldn't be fair.

"Chase?"

"Yeah?" I turned to face her.

"Your lips were really nice." She tucked a hair behind her ear. "I liked it." She smiled shyly again.

I was losing this battle. I slid my hands to both sides of her face and kissed her hard, abruptly. She responded willingly, arms wrapped around me, grasping tightly, nails grazing the bare skin of my back. I groaned as I sank against her, completely immersing myself. I didn't want to analyze why I was kissing her, I just wanted to do it . . . to lose myself with her these few moments. I was tired of feeling lonely. I needed to be with someone again, even if it was for all the wrong reasons.

I slid off the dock, into the cool water, pulling her

with me so we were out of view of the others, and I attacked her mouth again. She wrapped her arms around my neck, standing tiptoe to keep her head out of the water.

"Wrap your legs around me," I instructed, knowing I could hold her up easier.

"I have a better idea," she said, looking toward the boat. I watched as she climbed the step at the rear, and then followed after her. From one of the bench seats she pulled a blanket and laid it on the floor. She sat and patted the space next to her. "How's this?"

I grinned. "I like the way you think." I slipped down beside her, and she wrapped her arms around me again, and we moved together until I was lying on the floor with her above me.

We spent several breathless moments together, exploring the newness of one another before she slipped to my side and laid her head against my shoulder. I stared at the stars overhead as I tried to calm my breathing.

"That was fun," she whispered and I smiled.

"It was. Why'd you stop?"

"Because . . ." She hesitated. "I figured this is probably the first time you've kissed a girl since your . . . well . . . your girlfriend. I didn't want you to feel rushed into anything."

My thoughts instantly went—not to Nikki—but the burning kisses I'd shared with Brittney. The image of her lying on the bed beneath me was forever seared into my mind. I saw it every night before I fell asleep. This was probably *not* the time to bring that up.

"What're you thinking about?" she asked, shifting uncomfortably, and I scrambled to think of something.

"How much fun I've had today. It's been a long time coming."

She smiled and traced a finger in a circle over one

of my pecs before drawing down to my abs. "I hope I had something to do with that."

"You did." I grinned as I reached down, arresting her traveling finger and twisting it with my own. I took a deep breath, preparing to take the plunge. "How'd you like to do something with me next week? Maybe see a movie or something." I wasn't sure if I was really ready for this step, and I didn't know if she was the right person to take it with, but I figured it was the least I owed her after making out like we had. I wasn't sure if I was asking her for her, though, if she reminded me of Nikki—or if I was trying to forget about Brittney being currently wrapped in someone else's arms. I sighed. When did life get so complicated?

"I'd love to go out with you again. What day?"

Well, I was committed now. "Hmm. I have practice most afternoons, but we are usually done by six. Maybe Thursday at seven?"

"Thursday is perfect." She squeezed my fingers.

"What movie do you want to see?"

"I'll let you pick. Surprise me."

I chuckled. "Okay, but as you stated before, I'm rusty at this, so you can't be mad at me if I mess things up."

She laughed. "You won't. I can't imagine you messing anything up. You're too nice."

I eyed her down. "You should know I have serious issues with the word 'nice.' It usually doesn't mean anything good."

"Okay then, how about you're too sweet?"

I groaned. "You really aren't helping my ego."

She giggled and shifted so she was leaning over me. "All right. Then how about you're too much of a stud?"

"*Much* better." I grinned, and her lips met mine once again.

My mood was beyond foul today. I was currently releasing that aggression during practice drills. I stepped from the pocket and threw the ball as hard as I could toward the receiver, hitting him with a firm smack against his pads. He made another "oomph" sound, catching it this time, and started running the other direction.

Coach Bell blew the whistle. "Set it up again."

"Will you take it easy, Walker?" the receiver, Jared Webber, grumbled as he returned. "What crawled up your butt and died today? Geez."

"You take care of your job, and let me take care of mine," I snapped, grabbing another ball and getting into position.

He glared at me. "I could if you'd quit being such a damn diva."

I straightened shuffling the football between my hands and took a step toward him. "Well, if you'd learn how to catch *this* without dropping it sixty percent of the time, I wouldn't have to *teach* your pansy ass how it's done, now would I?"

He ran at me, lifting his fist into the air, but Brett and several others from the line stepped in front of me, keeping him away.

I grinned and continued tossing the ball as if I didn't have a care in the world. "Rule number one for the line. Never let them touch your quarterback. Sucks to be you right now, doesn't it?"

Jared struggled against the guys who held him, his face red with fury. "This is only practice. On this field you're just another stupid freshman—lower than shit. And no one has named you the quarterback yet."

I stared him square in the eye. "They will."

He shoved at Brett, pushing past. "Not if I kick your sorry punk ass so bad you can't play anymore."

He got within a foot of me before he was tackled to

the ground, spewing more foul obscenities for everyone to hear.

The coach blew his whistle loudly, and everyone stopped. I noticed Matt standing in the background, observing me with a scowl. I sent a sarcastic wink in his direction, and he flipped me off.

"Jared, you're excused to turn your gear in."

"What?" he bellowed, rage mottling his face. "You're kicking me off the team and not him?" He shoved a finger angrily in my direction.

"There's a no fighting policy on this team," the coach replied, standing his ground. "We know that there will occasionally be verbal disputes, but if you start throwing punches, you're done. Now go turn in your gear."

"I never hit him!" Jared yelled.

"You intended to. That's enough. I decide what works for my offense, and I want you off my field right now. You can go on your own, or I will call security. What's it going to be?"

I raised my eyebrows as I watched Coach Bell grow angrier. He was definitely intimidating, and as a burly ex-lineman himself, I certainly wouldn't be stupid enough to mess with him.

Jared apparently got the same impression, because he turned and strode toward the field exit. I didn't miss Matt clapping him on the shoulder in sympathy as he walked past.

"Walker!" Coach hollered.

"Yes, sir?" I said, snapping to attention as if I'd joined the Marines.

"Hit the bleachers, son, and don't stop running 'til I tell you it's okay!"

"Yes, sir!" I turned toward the stands. *Damn,* it was going to be a long night. Of course, I'd brought this on myself. Maybe a good exhausting run was exactly what I needed to adjust my attitude.

I couldn't help it. My mind had been a jumble of turmoil ever since I'd been at the lake. I shouldn't have made out with Jennifer, especially knowing any feelings of attraction I was having for her were most likely a direct result of her similarities to my dead girlfriend. Then I had to ask her out too, digging myself in deeper. She was going to think I was really into her.

If I was being honest, though, that wasn't bugging me the most. No, the problem was the fact that Brittney had caught me practically mauling Jennifer in the bottom of the boat and she hadn't seemed fazed by it for one second. She'd tried teasing me about it later, saying I certainly hadn't wasted any time getting my groove back. I realized she must honestly feel absolutely *nothing* but friendship for me. Here I was driving myself insane with visions of her twisted in my arms, and she was laughing at me. I was starting to wonder if she even remembered our shared kiss.

It burned—burned so badly it left a sour taste. The other thing that annoyed me was I wasn't sure when this had happened. Yes, I'd always thought Brittney attractive . . . okay, she was a knock out . . . but when did it become all about her? When did she become the primary thought in my head?

At night I would lie down in bed and stare at Nikki's smiling picture. I'd purposely started allowing myself to relive my memories with her—no matter how painful—hoping to find her in my dreams again. Instead, Brittney was blazoned through them, sometimes in all-consuming, passionate scenes that awakened me—on more than one occasion—in a sweat. I could feel my vision of Nikki starting to slip away—an almost tangible feeling of loss—as if she were sliding right through my fingers. I didn't want that to happen. I wanted to hang onto her with both hands and keep her here beside me, forever in my thoughts. I knew it wasn't possible. I knew our life together was over.

She was fading and I hated it. I was falling in love with someone else.

I didn't know what to do.

~Chapter Thirteen~

I tapped my fingers nervously against my pant leg as I approached the lobby desk of Jennifer's dorm. "What the hell are you doing here?" I mumbled to myself under my breath.

"I'm sorry?" the receptionist asked with a puzzled expression. "Did you say something?"

"I'm here to pick up Jennifer, uh," I fumbled to remember her last name, "Lucas. Jennifer Lucas, room 109."

"Please sign in here," she said, handing me a clipboard. "I also need to see some I.D."

I removed my wallet and showed her my driver's license. She nodded, and I signed the paper.

"Go through the double doors to your left, and 109 is on the ground floor, so continue past the elevators and down the hall."

"Thanks." I followed her instructions, and found the hall to be a crazy madhouse—girls running back and forth between the rooms in various states of dress. Doors were open, and music of all kinds was blaring loudly. It was complete chaos.

"Hey hottie. Please say you're here to see me." A curvy redhead with cute freckles leaned against her doorway. She checked me out in the most obvious way, her eyes stopping on specific regions of my body before returning to my face.

I couldn't help chuckling as I grinned back at her. "Actually, I'm looking for room 109."

She gave an exaggerated pout. "Bummer. Maybe

next time." She winked at me and gestured with her thumb. "Two doors down."

I nodded. "Have a good night."

She gave a little wolf whistle as I continued, and it was picked up by several others. A few girls peeked from their rooms to see what the commotion was. I shook my head. I could totally get behind living in a place like this.

The door swung open before I could knock, and Jennifer pulled me inside, quickly shutting it behind me. She took my breath away—her hair styled similar to Nikki's and then she smiled, looking even more like her. The resemblance was incredible, and all I wanted to do was kiss her and pretend she was.

"Did you survive the rabid dogs in the hall?" she asked with a giggle, the sound of her voice effectively ruining the illusion of Nikki in my mind. I glanced into her sparkling eyes, feeling like quite the jerk. She was a sweet girl. It wasn't her fault she looked like Nikki, and I shouldn't be using her this way, but I couldn't seem to help myself.

"I managed all right," I answered with a grin. "Only a few bite marks."

"Well then, I think you're lucky. I'm sure there are guys who've left this hall without their virtue intact."

A hard laugh rolled through me, caught by surprise at her choice of words. She was a funny girl. "I'm afraid my virtue wasn't intact before I walked through the door."

She gazed at me appreciatively. "Why doesn't that surprise me?"

"Are you ready to go?" I asked, not wanting to risk delving into my past any further.

"Yep," she replied, turning toward the two beds in the room, one of which had no bedding on it. "Let me grab my bag."

"You don't have a roommate?" I gestured at the bare side of the small space.

"Not yet. My old roommate left school at the end of last semester, and they didn't assign me another during the summer, which is fine with me. As you can see, it's hard to get peace and quiet around here. It's much worse during the regular school year."

I raised my eyebrows. "You're kidding."

She slipped her arm through mine, and guided me to the door. "Not in the least. Now don't worry. Hang onto my arm, Walker. I'll protect you."

I grinned as I followed after her.

We only suffered a few catcalls as we made our way through the rowdy hallway and into the lobby

"Why do I get the feeling you're a player?" she asked suddenly when we stepped outside.

"What do you mean?"

"I mean you look like you're enjoying this way too much."

I laughed again. "There was a time in my life when my dream might have been to live in a place exactly like this."

"So you're more of a buffet kind of guy then?"

"Like I said, that was another time. I don't mind dining on a single entrée these days." I winked at her.

"Well, that's good. I don't share well."

"Good to know." A sinking feeling in the pit of my stomach still irritated me. I might not be eating from any other dish, but that was only because the two courses I wanted weren't available. I was beyond low, but if Brittney wasn't interested, and Nikki was slipping away, why shouldn't I have someone to pass the time with? Everyone kept telling me I needed to get out and do something fun, and besides, I hadn't pursued her in the beginning. Brittney was the one who'd set us up. It wasn't my fault Jennifer happened to look like Nikki, and I hadn't decided to date her for that reason. It's not like I was going to marry her or anything. We were just two people chillin' together and having a good time.

"So what movie are we seeing?" Jennifer asked, breaking my moment of self-loathing and rationalization.

I shrugged. "I thought I'd let you pick. I figured we could hit a restaurant by Arizona Mills Mall and catch a movie afterward. If that sounds okay with you."

"It sounds fabulous."

I opened the truck door and waited for her to slip in, closing it behind her.

"Where do you want to eat?" I asked, when I climbed into the driver's seat.

"You decide since I'm choosing the movie."

"Do you like the Rainforest Cafe?"

"Is that the vine covered restaurant in the mall? I've never been, actually. It looks like a fun place, though."

"Well, I think I better rectify that then. Everyone should go there at least once."

"Let's do it."

We drove the short distance to the mall, and while waiting to be seated, admired the variety of fish swimming in the giant aquariums which twisted over our heads and down beside us.

"Look it's Nemo," I said, pointing to a clown fish. "And Dory," I added, pointing to another.

Jennifer started laughing.

"What?" I asked with a confused grin, unsure of what she found funny.

She shook her head, her eyes full of mirth. "I can't picture you watching Finding Nemo, let alone knowing anything about it."

"Ah." I took my cell phone from my pocket and clicked open my photo gallery, turning it so she could see the picture I pulled up. "This is Timmy and Clara."

"You have younger siblings?" She looked surprised.

"No." I shook my head and hurried to spit out the next few words. "Nikki, my girlfriend that died, this is her little brother and sister. They're the reason I've watched kid movies." I stared at the image, unable to help the smile on my face and the feeling that tugged at my heart. I missed them.

"They're adorable," she said leaning in for a closer look before glancing up. "So is this prior to her . . . passing?"

"After. I took this picture right before I moved down here. They were afraid I might forget them. As if that were possible."

"So you stay in touch with them a lot."

"They're like my second family. I've spent almost any free time I have with them and her mom."

"Wow. I bet that's difficult. It must be hard to be surrounded by her memory all the time."

"I want to remember her. I don't ever want to forget anything about her."

Disappointment flickered in Jennifer's eyes. "You're still in love with her, aren't you?"

"Walker, table for two?" the hostess called, saving me from answering. "Follow me right this way, please."

I deposited my phone in my pocket and placed my hand at the small of Jennifer's back, guiding her forward. We were seated near another fish tank, under part of the fiber-optic starry sky in the middle of the vine-draped restaurant.

"This is incredible," Jennifer said, as she gazed around.

"Just wait. It gets better," I replied, and as if on cue, crashing thunder rolled through the air, and animated jungle animals came to life around us; apes going wild, elephants trumpeting, cheetahs growling. An imitation of pouring rain began, heightening the sound of the giant waterfall in the middle of the room.

"What's happening?" Jennifer shouted above the noise, looking around with almost child-like glee.

"We're in the rainforest–it's raining." I smiled and she laughed.

"It's awesome!"

"I knew you'd like it."

"So does this make you Tarzan then?" She winked at me.

"Only if it means you're Jane," I flirted back.

"Do I get to see you in a loin cloth?"

My eyes widened at her brazen remark. "Will I be seeing *you* in one?"

"I'm afraid I don't own one."

Even in the darkness of the room I could see the blush stealing across her face.

"Such a sad day. I know I would've liked it. You worked that swimsuit of yours pretty well."

She laughed again, widely flashing the smile that was so much like Nikki's. In the dim light she resembled her even more. "Yours looked pretty good too."

"Thanks."

"The boat was my favorite part, though."

We hadn't spoken since we'd been at the lake. I'd worried things might be awkward between us, but it wasn't. I wondered if I found her easy to be with because she reminded me of Nikki.

"Maybe tonight we can find a new place to try something similar," I suggested.

"VOLCANO!" someone shouted loudly, and we both turned to see a waiter bringing a giant chocolate concoction layered with brownies and ice cream–a sizzling sparkler lit and firing at the top. He carried it past our table on the way to another.

Jennifer's eyes widened, and she turned to me. "We

must have one of those."

"As you wish," I said with a grin, and I signaled a waiter.

"Are you gonna come in?" Jennifer asked as we stood together in the now surprisingly quiet dorm hall. I couldn't believe it was the same wild and rowdy place we'd been a few hours ago.

I nodded. "Sure, if you'd like."

"I'd like."

During our evening together I'd been very restrained. I was polite enough, and we joked a lot. At one point she reached over and held my hand. It felt nice enough, and I tried to relax and enjoy it—live in the moment—but my mind kept drifting to the other two girls in my life. I caught myself wondering several times during the movie what Brittney might be up to this evening and if she was perhaps on a date somewhere herself. And I thought of Nikki every time I looked at Jennifer, even though I really tried not to.

Jennifer grabbed my hand and pulled me through the door. I shut it behind us, and she tossed her purse onto a small, organized desk on her side of the room before turning to face me again. She grabbed both of my hands and stepped backward, leading me toward the bed. "How's this location for a repeat performance?"

"Looks pretty good to me."

She sat on the bed, releasing my hands and wrapping her arms around my neck as she lay back, pulling me down. I settled in easily, my body fitting well against hers, and I brushed my lips across hers.

"I've been wanting you to do this all night," Jennifer sighed. "I was beginning to wonder if it was ever going to happen."

"Sorry I kept you waiting so long." I stared at her beautiful mouth, thinking of another's, and I kissed her again, this time harder, aggressively. I kissed her like I wished I could with *her*—Brittney, not Nikki—surprising myself.

I could remember the feel of her beneath me, but I roughly attempted to shove it from my mind, trying to be in the here and now, attempting to feel and kindle that spark I desperately wanted.

This girl was real, and she wanted *me*, not someone else. She liked being with *me*. She wanted to kiss *me*. I owed her the same respect.

I kissed my way down into the crook of her neck, nuzzling and sucking there, listening to her increased breathing. Her body arched underneath me, signaling she wanted more, and her hands slid under my shirt, pushing it out of the way.

"Wait," I said, lifting away. "Wait." I couldn't believe I was the one calling a halt to this.

"What is it?" Jennifer asked, confused.

"I'm sorry. I . . ." my voice trailed off as I studied her face, searching for a way to tell her what was going on inside me. She was such a pretty girl, and sweet too. I honestly wished I could get over myself.

"It's too soon for you, isn't it?' she asked, reaching up to brush her palm across my cheek. "I didn't mean to push. After last weekend, I thought maybe you were ready to move on."

"I want to move on." I tipped my head, leaning into her hand and rubbing affectionately against it. "I'm trying, but I guess it's something I can't force. I'm sorry. I know we were pretty hot and heavy last weekend, so this must sound strange to you now."

She continued to stroke me comfortingly. "No it doesn't. You know the old saying, I'm sure—the heart wants what the heart wants."

She was exactly right. That was my problem. My heart wanted someone else, but she didn't want me.

"Can we keep dating?" she asked. "We can take things slower. Is that okay?"

"Yes," I responded, wondering what the heck I was saying.

"Let's go out again . . . tomorrow," she suggested. "My treat this time."

"Sound great." I kissed her briefly and got off her. "I better go home now. Thanks for trying to understand." I knew she didn't understand at all.

"Don't worry about it. Everything will work out." She sounded so sure.

"Hopefully." I gave a small smile and headed toward the door. "See you tomorrow."

~Chapter Fourteen~

I wandered around the edges of the clearing, fading in and out amongst the edges of the pine trees, quietly observing my mother and her new husband from a distance. Her laughter would often rise up, tinkling on the gentle breeze as she mingled through the reception tables, visiting with her guests. She was on Greg's arm, and he was unable to take his eyes off her. I was hard pressed to remember her ever being this light hearted.

That made me a little sad, actually. I thought back to our old life and her relationship with my dad. I'd always believed they were extremely happy together. True, he was gone a lot on business, and I was away most of the time with my activities, so I didn't see them together as often, but I couldn't really remember a time she seemed this carefree. Greg was good for her.

The wedding had been beautiful, small and intimate, with our closest family and friends. It had been strange watching my mom come down the makeshift aisle as I stood next to Greg. The mountain location they'd chosen in Greer made the perfect place to celebrate a new union together, he in a nice black suit, she in a very slim-cut white, satin dress. They exchanged their vows in front of a clear, sparkling fork in the Colorado River. My mom had wanted something to symbolize a fresh new start and show her embracing her new mountain home. I think she'd gotten exactly what she was hoping for. I was happy for her.

I sighed, taking a moment to shrug off my suit coat and loosen my tie before leaning against the base of a towering Ponderosa. If only I could figure out how to bring happiness back into my life again, I'd have it made. My mom was proof things could turn around, but I didn't know how to apply it to me.

My gaze naturally found Brittney amongst the guests, and I watched her as she smiled and laughed at the table where she sat with Brett, Tana, and a few of our other friends. She'd been going out with Jeff almost every day since we'd gone to the river. It drove me insane.

True, I'd dated Jennifer and had a great time with her as well. Yes, we'd proven there was some physical chemistry between us, spending a lot of time making out together, but I couldn't stop feeling guilty about it. There were too many extenuating circumstances to let my guard down. Did I like her for her, for Nikki, or because I didn't have Brittney? I honestly didn't know. Being with her was a comfort, for sure, but deep down something still ate and nagged at me.

I didn't think I was ready for this. Trying to throw myself back into the living world was becoming more than I could take. I knew people were concerned for me, and they wanted my happiness as well, but in truth, I was still mourning for a past I'd never have again . . . and now I felt like the one person I could move forward with would never be available to me. I was stuck in limbo between the two things I desired most, unable to grasp either of them.

In that instant, one thing became glaringly obvious. There was no place for Jennifer in my life. She was too sweet of a girl for me to lead on because I was lonely. I needed to break things off with her when I got home . . . hopefully in a kind enough manner we could still remain friends. I didn't want to hurt her.

Making the decision was half the battle apparently, because a sudden wave of calm came over me. This was the right thing to do, I was sure of it. Now I just needed to, once again, focus my attention on football. Maybe that would keep me distracted enough from the other things going on in my life.

Straightening, I threw my jacket over my shoulder and headed down the edge of the creek, meandering slowly as I tried to immerse myself in the nature surrounding me. I redirected my thoughts to old fishing and camping trips I'd taken occasionally with my dad or my grandpa when I was younger. Those had been relaxed days—feeling the soft breeze whisper through the pine needles, smelling the fresh mountain air, laughing together as we excitedly pulled fish after fish out of the water. My mouth watered remembering some of the delicious fish fries we'd had afterward. I missed doing things like that.

My thoughts were interrupted by the sound of someone walking up behind me, and I turned to see Brittney approaching. My heart leapt, but I only gave her a small smile and returned my focus to the creek, laying my jacket on a waterside picnic table.

"Hey, Rockstar. What're you doing wandering around by yourself?" she asked.

I grinned. "Worried I'm gonna get lost in the forest?"

"You? Never. I could see you stripping down to take a swim, though." She smiled and I laughed.

"Yeah, my mom would kill me if I did that today."

"Most likely." She came along beside me and linked her arm through mine. "We haven't had many chances to talk lately. How're things going? I hear you've been going out a lot with Jennifer."

I raised my eyebrows. "From who?"

"From Jennifer, duh. She can't stop talking about what a great kisser you are."

I sighed. What a mess. I didn't want Brittney

thinking things were getting hot and heavy with Jennifer. "She's a nice girl."

"Uh oh."

"What?"

"You just said nice. I know how you feel about that word. You're not gonna stop seeing her are you?"

I nodded, staring into the rushing water. "I think it would be for the best. I don't want to lead her on." I looked up to see how she was taking the news, searching for anything that would tell me she was glad about this development, but she frowned instead.

"I thought she was good for you. It's the first time you've seemed happy in ages."

"She was good for me. Getting to know her helped me straighten a few things out in my head—but I feel like I'm using her. I think I'm attracted to her because she reminds me of Nikki. That's not fair. She needs someone to like her for her."

She paused before patting me on the arm. "I'm pleased you don't want to take advantage. You've always had a good, strong sense of character."

I snorted. "You really don't know me that well, do you?"

She arched an eyebrow. "I think I know you very well."

"If you did, you wouldn't be saying that. Character has never been my strong point."

"No, I disagree. I think character has always been your strong point. You wouldn't be here otherwise. Quit looking at the things in your life from a negative standpoint. Do you realize the tragedies you've overcome—the hardships? You standing here now is a tribute to the kind of character you have."

"If you say so."

"I do, and we both know . . . I'm always right." She grinned, lifting her chin a bit as if she were daring me to contradict.

"I'll let you win—this time. I'm not in the mood to argue today." I glanced farther down the slightly visible trail we were standing on. "Walk with me for a while? I just wanna chill and enjoy the day, but I'm not really feeling the whole crowd thing right now."

"I always love hanging out with you. You know that. Anytime, anywhere—all you have to do is say the word and I'm there." She gripped my arm tighter.

"Really?" I asked, wondering if she was serious.

"Really, Chase. You're one of my very best friends. I'd do anything for you."

It wasn't a declaration of love by any means, but I was willing to take her up on it. Maybe if we spent more time together she'd see me in a different light and things would naturally develop between us. It was worth a shot.

"I'm glad you're in my life, Brittney. I don't think you realize exactly how much it means to have you there." I slipped my hand over and intertwined my fingers through hers. It didn't appear to bother her that I wanted to hold her hand while we walked together. The path was uneven, scattered with rocks and large clumps of heavy natural grasses. She was wearing dress shoes, and I didn't want her to fall.

"You look very pretty today, by the way." I glanced from the top of her head over the pale pink halter dress she was wearing which showed off her sun-kissed skin and delicious looking curves. I decided to go for the safer topic. "I've never seen you wear your hair that way before."

She shrugged. "I thought it would be fun to do it fancier for the wedding."

I watched the small tendrils brushing against her neck and cheeks, escaping the messy loose bun adorned with tiny dried flowers. I wanted to brush those places as well.

"Again, it's very pretty. But you always look that way, I guess."

She squeezed my hand and laughed. "Now I know why Nikki fell so hard for you. You're a good sweet talker."

I smiled. "Not trying to sweet talk. Simply stating the facts." Okay, maybe I was trying to sweet talk a little. I wanted her to notice me.

She laughed. "Whatever. Admit it. You're putting that Chase Walker flirt on me hardcore. I know how you are."

"If I was flirting with you, you'd *know* it."

"Are you sure about that?"

"Positive."

"Hmmm." She sounded doubtful.

I abruptly yanked on her hand, causing her to stumble forward, and caught her against me. I slipped my free arm around her waist, holding her there. Our faces were only inches apart as I stared down, and she looked at me with wide eyes. I released her hand, lifting mine to lightly stroke the side of her face, trailing my fingers to her neck and dipping lightly into the hollow at her throat. Her pulse was beating rapidly under her skin, and her breathing increased.

I leaned forward, closer to her slightly gaping mouth, my lips descending before pausing, our breath mingling together. "Can you feel me flirting now?" I whispered, nudging the tip of her nose with my own.

She swallowed hard. "Uh . . . , maybe."

"Don't tempt me to go farther, Brittney, unless you mean it."

"Why not?"

"Because you *are* a girl I could lose myself in," I replied honestly.

Her lips pressed into a firm line, and she took a step

away.

Rejected again. "What's the matter?" I tried to put a teasing quality into my voice to diffuse the sudden awkwardness of the situation. "Are you chicken?"

She shook her head. "No," she said flatly, not breaking eye contact.

"Then what is it?"

She reached up and tugged on her earlobe nervously, glancing around quickly before settling her gaze on me once again. "I can't be a rebound for you, Chase. I know you like me because I'm easy for you to be with. You know me already. But I won't risk our friendship over a quick fling with you."

"Who said anything about a quick fling?" I asked, a wave of exasperation rolling through me.

"No one needs to. Anyone can plainly see your heart is not in it."

"You have no idea what my heart is feeling."

"Then why don't you tell me?"

I could do that. "Do you know what I've been going through since we kissed? Do you know how often it plays over and over again in my head? It's like a broken record—but you act like it didn't faze you in the least. You picked up and moved on with another guy without blinking an eye. Why would you do that?"

"You called me Nikki, Chase! You weren't kissing me . . . , you were kissing her! I can't and won't compete with a ghost. She'll never be anything but perfect in your eyes. Don't you see? You'll constantly be comparing us, and I'll be the one who always comes up short. I love her, and I love you, but I love *me* too much to put myself through a disaster like that! If it means all you and I can ever be together is friends, then fine. As long as you're still in my life—I'm okay with that."

I stood there, stock still, trying to absorb everything she'd just said, wishing I knew the right words to say to make her see.

"I'm not okay with that," I finally muttered. "I want—"

"You want Nikki. I get it. I'm sorry her death has damaged you so badly. If I could bring her back to you, I would. I want you to be happy."

I reached and grasped her by the hand. "You're not listening to me, Brittney. Please, hear me out for one minute."

She waited, and again I was at a loss for words. I stepped closer and traced her lips with my thumb and finally decided to be straight with her. "I think *you* could be the one who makes me happy." I felt her breath intake at my words, and I hurried to continue. "I'm sorry I called you her name, and I'm sorry I raced out of there like that. You're right, I've been very confused, but I told you that being with Jennifer helped me clear something up. That something was you. I don't want to be with her . . . even if she reminds me of Nikki. It's you I can't stop thinking about."

I searched her eyes for an indication of how she was feeling, hoping I was getting through.

"I don't know, Chase," she finally said. "Everything is so complicated. I believe you care for me, but I know how you love her too. That's a lot for a girl to get past."

I dropped my hand and stepped back. "I'm sorry. I shouldn't have told you all this." I felt my hopes beginning to shatter.

She placed her hand on my arm. "No, I'm glad you did. It'll help me understand things better. I think I'm going to need some . . . time, I guess—a little space to consider what you've told me."

I gave a strangled laugh. "Take all the time you need. I've got nowhere to be."

"Don't talk like that. Don't go all pity party on me. You've got great things to look forward to, and you know it. Your career in football is starting to take off. There are big things ahead of you."

"Football makes a damn cold bed partner, Britt," I snapped.

She looked up, shocked. "Is that where you want me to step up?"

"The thought has crossed my mind, yes."

"Chase . . . ,"

"And before you start filling your head with anymore lies of this being about Nikki, you might want to consider one thing."

"What's that?" she asked, confused.

"Nikki was never in my bed."

Her eyes widened, and she fidgeted nervously with her hair, my meaning apparent. She cleared her throat. "I see. Um, I think it'd be best to head back to the reception now." She started walking in the direction we'd just come.

"Britt," I called, and she glanced over her shoulder. "Give it to me straight, right now. Is there any hope at all for you and me?"

She stared at the ground for a moment, kicking at a pebble with the toe of her shoe before looking up again. "I can't profess to know what the future holds, but I do know one thing I've learned in my life —there's always hope, Chase. There's always hope." She smiled ever so slightly and walked away, but my heart lifted as if it were on wings.

She didn't say no. It was a fragile offer, but an offer nonetheless. I followed her to the reception, sitting by my grandpa at one of the tables and then visiting with Nikki's mom before playing a rambunctious game of tag with Timmy and Clara.

I didn't get another chance to talk to Brittney alone, but she would often look over and give me a quick smile as she chatted with other guests. It significantly warmed my heart, and suddenly things seemed like they were looking up.

~Chapter Fifteen~

My mood was drastically less positive by the end of the following week. My carefully explained reasons for calling things to a halt with Jennifer hadn't been well received at all. She couldn't grasp why I wanted to call it quits when we seemed to have such good chemistry. When I finally got frustrated and blurted out she reminded me of my dead girlfriend—well, it had been entirely the wrong thing to say. She'd stormed away that night, leaving me standing alone in the parking lot outside her uncle's restaurant.

I'd seen Brittney watching our exchange through the window with a sorrowful expression on her face. I was unable to stop staring until she gave a shrug and shook her head, returning to work.

I went home and waited up for her, hoping she'd come talk to me, but she didn't. I lay on my bed rolling a football between my hands as I listened to sounds from her room on the other side of the wall. She had her music playing, and I wondered what else she might be doing. She was so close, but still so far away.

Things went from nerve-wracking to downright unbearable when I passed Brittney as she left with Jeff, not one, but two nights during the week. It was all I could do to force a smile and be cordial when Jeff paused to ask me about football, casually draping his arm around Britt's shoulders. I imagined what it would feel like to punch him in the face without any warning, and my fists curled of their own accord, forcing me to call an abrupt end to the conversation and hurry into my apartment. I was losing it.

"What's up with you these days?" Brett asked as I rammed into the sleds after practice.

"What do you mean?" I gasped as I charged and hit them again.

"I mean you're not a lineman, Chase. Why are you doing this? Besides, practice is over." He waved his arm around the tented, air-conditioned practice field. "Everyone is gone. We're the last two people here. Let's go home. I'm hungry."

"Go ahead," I grunted. "I'm not stopping you. I'll run home."

"Dude, you drove. What the hell is eating you so badly? I swear you've been on your damn period for a week now!"

I stopped; snorting as I laughed. "You seriously did not just go there."

"Yes, I did." He came over and grabbed my shoulder pads, turning me toward the locker rooms. "You're acting worse than my sister."

The thought of Britt made me sigh in frustration. "I'll be fine. Just trying to work through some stuff."

"When did you become such a wuss?"

"Excuse me?"

"You're not the Chase I used to know—the guy who never let anything stand in his way. You wanted something—you went and got it. Don't you remember how you chased Nikki down until she finally gave in? Now you sit around acting moody all the time. I mean, I know you've been through hell and back, but you're worse than a mopey dang girl these days. I don't know how much longer I can take it."

"I'm not *that* bad," I grumbled.

"Dude you were listening to love songs by the Backstreet Boys in your room last night."

"It was an old playlist mix Nikki made for me," I

said defensively, and he rolled his eyes. I sighed, relenting. "Fine, I give up. I may have been acting a little grumpy lately."

"A little?" He raised his eyebrows. "I've been ready to call your mom and tell her she should come talk to you."

"Don't do that. She's only been married a week. Let her enjoy it. I'll be fine."

"How do I know that? Are you going to do something about it?"

"About what?" I asked, confused.

Brett shook his head. "About Brittney. Are you going to mope around, or are you going to man up and get your girl."

I was shocked. "How do you know this has anything to do with Brittney?"

"Blind, dead dogs can see you have a thing for her, bro. Every time the two of you get within twenty feet of each other it's like the air starts lighting up with electricity. What's the hold up? Get it over with, and put the rest of us out of our misery. Besides, it'd be fun to double date together."

"It's not gonna happen."

"Why not?"

"Have you talked to your sister about any of this?"

He shook his head. "No. She's as tight lipped about things as you are. What's going on?"

"She doesn't want me," I stated bluntly, as I pulled my gear over my head as we walked into the locker room.

"Bull."

I shrugged, reaching to undo my practice pants. "Believe it or not, it's your choice. I tried talking to her about it, and she said she didn't feel like it was a good thing. She thinks I'll constantly compare her to Nikki, and she'll be competing against a ghost that'll always be perfect in my eyes."

Sitting on the bench, I took my shoes and socks off before grabbing a towel and heading to the showers, not waiting for Brett's reply. I turned the water on as hot as I could stand it and let it sluice over my skin as I braced against the wall, trying to relax my tight muscles. I hurt everywhere—inside and out—and I couldn't help thinking some blunt would be the perfect thing right now to take the edge off.

I only allowed myself to entertain the thought for a few seconds before forcing myself to move on to the subject of food and what sounded good for dinner. I was getting dang sick of pizza lately. It seemed like that's all Brett and I ever ate these days.

"Let's go eat somewhere good tonight," I hollered to Brett as I grabbed the soap and started washing off.

"Like where?" he answered loudly from wherever he was.

"I don't care, as long as it's not pizza!"

"Wanna go to that restaurant Britt works at?"

"No!" I said forcefully. "Jennifer works there, and she's pissed at me right now. I'd probably end up with a razor blade in my food or something. We should probably avoid that place for a while."

"How about The Devil's Pit then?"

"As long as Matt isn't there. I think it's his preferred hangout now. I can't eat if I have to look at him."

"Dude, if you're gonna keep burning bridges, can you stop doing it with peeps from our favorite restaurants?"

I laughed. "The Devil's Pit is fine. If Matt's there I'll punch him in the face and throw him out the door. It'll improve the environment."

"So I should plan on dinner in jail is that what you're saying?"

I scoffed. "Would I do that to you?"

"Yes, I believe you would."

I grinned, turning off the water and grabbing a towel to dry before tucking it around my waist. I emerged from the shower to find Brett leaving one a few stalls down. As we approached the lockers, Coach Bell walked in, looking between the two of us solemnly.

"Have either of you been outside recently?" he asked.

I shook my head. "No, we've been on the practice field, why?"

"Get dressed and meet me outside," he said, heading toward the door.

"Wonder what that's all about?" Brett muttered.

"I have no idea, but he didn't look too happy, did he?"

"Nope."

When we were clothed, we grabbed our equipment bags and headed into the hall, making our way to the parking lot. Coach Bell was waiting by the front door as we stepped out.

"What's up, Coach?" I asked, waiting for him to fill us in.

He pointed to the lot. "Isn't that yours?"

I glanced in the direction he indicated. "What the hell?" I dropped my bag on the sidewalk and ran toward my truck—*my truck*—smashed up by a baseball bat from the looks of it.

My eyes watered as I stared at the last gift I'd received from my dad before he died. All the windows were busted, the headlights had been bashed in and huge gouging dents covered the body.

"Who would do this?" Brett asked, joining me, his jaw gaping.

"I've called the cops. They should be here any minute," Coach said as he walked up. "Hopefully they can find some eye witnesses. This is extensive damage.

It would've taken someone a while to do it."

"Unless it was more than one person, "Brett added.

I peered inside, the upholstery slashed, and wires were dangling from the gaping hole where my stereo used to be. Even the tires were flat.

"Don't touch anything," Coach said. "The police might be able to find fingerprints or something."

I closed my eyes, the image of my dad standing on the carport the morning of my birthday flashed in front of me, and it was as if someone had sucker punched me—ripping away my last good memory of him. I couldn't stop shaking with rage. If I ever discovered who did this, they were going to be in severe danger of ending up like my truck.

~Chapter Sixteen~

There was a soft knock at my bedroom door, but I ignored it. I wasn't in the mood to talk to anyone right now. I lay still in the dark, not making a sound, hoping whoever it was would think I was already asleep and go away.

I bit back a groan as the knock came again. "Chase?" Brittney's voice spoke.

I wondered what she wanted, but I didn't answer.

The door opened a crack, and I watched as she poked her head in, the fixture from the hallway backlighting her and making her blonde hair glow like she was an angel.

"Chase?"

"You're taking a big risk coming in here like this." I released a sigh. "What if I'd been laying here naked?"

She shrugged. "What if you had? Do you sleep naked often?"

I snorted. "Nah, not really."

"I didn't think so. Can I come in?"

"If you don't mind sitting in the dark. I have a blinding headache right now."

She stepped the rest of the way inside, leaving the door open a crack as she came to stand beside the edge of the bed. "Scoot over. I want to lay down next to you."

My pulse sped up even though I didn't want it to. I did as she asked, moving closer to the wall. She stretched out and cuddled against me, laying her head on my shoulder, then wrapping an arm and leg across the top of me. My arms went around her voluntarily.

"What brought this on?" I asked, completely confused.

"I thought you might need a hug."

"So you're copping a pity feel then?" I didn't like that. "I don't need you to be sorry for me, Britt."

She embraced me tighter. "I'm sorry about your truck, yes, but that's not why I came."

My pulse picked up. "Why did you?"

"I realized today that I miss you. I don't like the awkwardness between us right now, and I don't like knowing I've hurt you."

I pondered this for a moment, loving the way she felt in my arms—different, but good all the same. I squeezed her lightly. "I'm trying to understand. I know you can't help how you feel."

"That's just it. I'm pushing you away for the wrong reasons. It's not because I'm not attracted to you—I am. It's because I'm scared of what you might do to my heart if it doesn't work."

"What are you saying, Britt?" I held my breath, hoping.

"I'm saying I want to date you . . . if you still want me." In the small shaft of light from the doorway, I could see her biting her lip.

My breath came in a rush of relief as I hugged her tighter, nestling my chin into her hair. "I still want you." I was soaring on cloud nine. I hadn't felt this happy since . . . Nikki. I shoved that thought to the back of my mind. "What made you change your mind?"

She made an ironic laughing sound. "Jeff actually."

This surprised me. "What? How?"

She sighed. "Every time I've been with him this week I've compared him to you. I look at him and think about how he looks next to you. I watch what he does, and I wonder if you would do it that way. It finally occurred to me that he wasn't the person I wanted to be with all the time. You were."

"So did you talk to him about it?"

"I did."

"And?"

"He said you seemed like a decent guy, and he wouldn't hold any grudges."

"Remind me to send him a Christmas card this year." I grinned. "So, what now?"

"Now we take it slow, Chase, and I mean almost painfully slow. There's no need to rush things. Let's date and see what happens. I don't want to force something that might not be there."

"And by slow you mean . . . ?"

"No throwing me on your bed and making out with me while you're peeling my clothes off. I don't even want there to be kissing right now. Let's really get to know each other better before we start throwing a bunch of hormones into the mix, okay? You owe it to yourself. You're coming from a difficult place, and I want you to be sure about things. Really sure."

"I'm not gonna take advantage and run away. You can trust me."

"I do trust you, otherwise I wouldn't be here. But I've come from a bad relationship too. I need time to heal as well. Can you do this for me?"

I sighed. "I'll try, but it's gonna be awfully hard if you keep crawling into my bed like this."

"Then I'll go. I wanted you to know how I felt, though."

She rolled away, and I missed her instantly. My first instinct was to grab her back, but I knew if I did I'd be pushing her conditions. I was ready to make out with her the entire night. I didn't want to scare her away again, though. She was definitely scared and fragile.

I watched her as she slipped through the door.

"Brittney," I called, and she poked her head in

again.

"Yeah?"

"Thank you." I couldn't help my smile.

"Good night, Chase."

I woke the next morning, full of energy, refreshed and ready to start a new day. I hopped out of bed and hurried to the shower across the hall, singing to myself as I went. When I was finished, I went into Brett's room.

"Hey dude. Can I borrow your car for a while this morning? My rental won't be ready until noon."

"Keys are on the dresser," he mumbled into his pillow.

"Thanks, man. You're the best! I won't be gone long."

He lifted his head slightly and squinted at me with one eye. "Why are you up this early, and why are you so dang chipper?"

I grinned. "It's a beautiful day outside. Time to start living." I headed toward the door.

Brett sat up and stared at me. "Now you're scaring me."

I chuckled. "Brittney came to visit me last night."

"And?"

I shrugged. "And we're going to date. She wants to take things slow, but I'm okay with that. Some is better than none, right?"

He smiled. "I'm glad she's coming around." He paused, watching me for a moment before continuing. "Happy looks good on you."

"I agree. I feel good for the first time in . . . ," A bit of regret shot through me. "Is it bad that I don't feel guilty? I feel guilty because I don't feel guilty. Is that okay?" I didn't know if I was making any sense.

"You want my honest opinion?" he asked, solemnly.

"Let's hear it."

"I think Nikki, wherever she is, is probably clapping her hands with joy seeing the smile on your face. She'd be devastated knowing how badly you've suffered because of her. I've always thought she'd want you to be happy."

I mulled his comment over, remembering the recent dream I'd had about her. "It's been hard to let go. I still love her so much."

"No one expects you to stop loving her, Chase. You can keep those feelings with you for the rest of forever. But think about it . . . what if it had been you that died? Would you want her to sit around and suffer for the rest of her life?"

"No." I didn't even have to ponder on it. "I'd want her to be happy too, even if it was without me. I love her."

"Then why do you keep torturing yourself? Take your own advice, and assume she'd feel the same way. Keep loving her—love the things she gave you—those are yours to keep. It's okay to open your heart and share it with someone else too. You and Britt—well, I think you'd work really well together. You should see where it might go."

I grinned again. "When did you get so smart?"

"When I had to watch my best friend agonize over his broken heart, and I couldn't do anything about it."

"I'm sorry I've been difficult to live with. I swear, I've been trying to get past things, I'm just not really sure how to do it."

"Well, I think you're on the right track. I say keep doing whatever you're doing right now. You're . . . glowing." He snickered.

"You're a dork. Fresh muffins . . . that's what's making me "glow." I'm going to pick some up and surprise your sister with breakfast. It won't be my grandma's muffins, but I figure it'll do in a pinch. You want some?"

"No, Tana wants to do something with me later. Thanks though."

"All right. Catch ya in few then."

I left the apartment, my heart feeling lighter than it had in months. I wasn't sure how things were going to work out, but for the first time in ages I was truly excited for the future.

I knocked loudly on the door and waited, box of baked goods in hand. After a minute, I frowned and knocked again. There was still no answer, so I tried the knob. I shook my head when I found it unlocked again, and I opened the door a crack.

"Hello?" I called. There was no answer, but I could hear the shower running and the girls carrying on a conversation.

I stepped inside, going to the kitchen counter and searching for a piece of paper and a pen, so I could leave a note. I peeked around the corner and saw the bathroom door open. Tana was sitting on the sink talking to Brittney.

"I bet you're excited," Tana said.

"I am," Brittney's voice came from behind the shower curtain, which did nothing to help my rabid imagination. "I've always liked him, Tana, but he was Nikki's guy from the get go, and I was with Matt. I never thought of him as someone I'd be with."

They were talking about me. I froze in place, unable to resist eavesdropping.

"We've been friends for a long time," she continued, "and I'm kind of afraid to tamper with that, but something is different now. I honestly can't stop thinking about him."

I grinned to myself. The feeling was mutual.

"I know he's always liked you. You two get along really well together. It seems like a no-brainer to me. It's only natural you'd be drawn to one another."

"Maybe it's just weird because . . . you know . . . he's Nikki's."

My heart fell, and I faltered. *Am I really doing the right thing?*

"Nikki loved you both, and she hated Matt if I can remind you. I think if she knew there was no way she and Chase could ever be together, she'd be thrilled two of the people she loved most found each other."

"Really?" Brittney replied, and I thought I heard her release a strangled sound. "Because this has been a really hard decision for me. I feel like I'm stabbing her in the back and trying to steal her boyfriend—like I'm betraying her memory."

Emotions swirled around me. I might be on the other side of this situation, but I understood exactly what she meant.

"Don't feel that way. I think she'd tell you to go for it. She'd want you to be happy."

"Would you feel that way if it was Brett we were talking about."

Tana was quiet for several moments. "I'd like to think I would," she finally replied. "But the fact of the matter is, Nikki's dead, and Chase has no future with her. They are done and over with. He needs to move on, and so do you."

I was starting to feel sick. Eavesdropping wasn't such a good idea after all. I hated hearing Nikki's and my relationship discussed so bluntly. I turned toward the door, leaving the muffins on the counter.

"I want to move on, Tana. He does funny things to me."

I paused, curious about what she meant.

"Funny things?" Tana asked.

"To my body." She laughed. "Like how my stomach drops as if I were on a roller coaster every time I see him, or my pulse races whenever he touches me."

Okay, I could stay and listen for a minute longer, I edged closer to the bathroom.

Tana laughed. "I can see how that happens. Chase is hot!"

"He really is. He came home from practice the other night without his shirt on, and I almost died. I wanted to run my hands all over him."

"You should've, I wouldn't have stopped you," I said as I leaned against the doorway, and both girls screamed.

"What are you doing?" Tana said, holding her hand to her chest.

"I brought breakfast. You two need to start locking your door. Anyone could walk right in."

"How much did you hear?" Brittney asked, sounding horrified.

"I heard enough." I chuckled as I folded my arms. "Please feel free to continue. I find the discussion to be quite stimulating."

"Get out!" she ordered, and Tana jumped off the counter and pushed me out the door.

"But I brought you breakfast, and I want to hear what else you have to say," I hollered as I struggled with Tana. "You were talking about rubbing your hands all over me. Please go on!"

She growled, and Tana continued shoving me down the hall. "Go home!" she ordered.

"Okay, okay. You don't have to be snotty about it. I'm leaving." I pointed to the box on the counter. "There's breakfast. And lock your door!"

She smiled at me as I left, and I couldn't stop grinning. That was fun.

~Chapter Seventeen~

I was still grinning when Britt walked into the apartment fifteen minutes later carrying the box.

"For someone who preaches locking the door, you might wish to follow your own advice."

"I'm a guy, it's different."

"Wow, that's sexist."

I shrugged. "It's the truth."

"If a burglar came in here and shot you, you'd die as easily as I would." She gave me an arched look. "We aren't in Silver Creek anymore."

"Point taken." I couldn't take my eyes off her—she was beautiful—wet hair combed straight, no makeup, and wearing a form-fitting tank top and shorts which showed her perfect figure and luminescent skin. I wanted to touch her—everywhere.

"Thank you for breakfast, but I wanted to share it with you."

"That was my initial plan, before I was roughly thrown from your apartment. Have a seat." I gestured to the spot on the couch, and she came to join me.

"This was very sweet of you. I love blueberry muffins." She opened the box and handed one to me.

"I know. I remember Nikki, Tana, and you used to get them all the time from the bakery."

She smiled softly. "It's a wonder we weren't a bunch of lard butts. I miss doing things like that with the two of them. Nikki's gone and Tana spends most of her time with Brett. I always feel like a third wheel when I tag along."

"So what do you say to starting some new traditions? Maybe Muffin Mondays with your new boyfriend? It'll give you something to look forward to."

Her smile grew wider. "I have a new boyfriend? I thought we were just dating."

"Hmmm. That does change things, doesn't it? I was under the impression you and I were going to date exclusively. I don't know if I'm the sharing type."

She giggled. "I'm only messing with you. I wanted to see what you'd say." She popped a piece of muffin into her mouth.

I slid my arm behind her on the sofa and leaned in real close, my forehead almost touching hers. "Don't tease me, Brittney, I'm still too fragile," I whispered seriously. "I don't want you to date anyone else, only me, exclusive—*I* want to be your boyfriend."

Her breath stilled, and she quit chewing, swallowing as my lips brushed against the side of her face. She closed her eyes and tilted her head as I feathered lightly down to the pulse point in her neck.

A small moan escaped her, and I pulled away slightly. Her eyes flew open and she stared at me. "Why'd you stop?"

I grinned. "Who's your boyfriend?"

"You are," she replied without hesitation.

I kissed her neck again, and she sighed, smiling. I didn't want to stop, but I knew she wanted to be careful, so I moved away.

She gave an exasperated huff. "Why'd you stop this time?"

"Because *my girlfriend* told me she wanted to take things slowly. Slow is not gonna happen if I keep touching you like this. Regardless of how things ended up the last time we kissed, my body can't help but remember the feel of you underneath me, and it's kinda anxious for a repeat performance. If you know what I mean." I arched an eyebrow.

Her eyes widened and she blushed. "I know what you mean."

"Good. Now eat your muffin." I broke a piece off and held it up to her mouth. She grinned slyly and took it, licking and sucking at the tips of my fingers in the processes. I groaned. "You aren't playing fair, Britt."

"Neither are you, getting me all hot and bothered with your kisses. I was only returning the favor."

"Keep it up and you're gonna land flat on your back."

"Why do I think you're being completely serious?"

"Because I am. If I had my way I'd throw you over my shoulder right now and carry you off into the other room."

"Boys and their hormones," she muttered. "Always raging."

I laughed. "What do you expect when you girls keep driving us crazy with your maddening, sexy, antics."

"Can you not molest my twin while I'm in the same house and within hearing distance?" Brett asked, wandering in and plopping in the chair before reaching for the box of muffins. His blond hair was poking up all over the place, and he scratched his head, blinking rapidly like he was still trying to wake up.

Britt and I both laughed. "I'm afraid I can't promise that, no," I replied, the mood effectively broken. "Besides, I thought you were thrilled I was going to be molesting your sister."

"As bad as that sounds, I am thrilled about it. I can't think of anything better than my twin hooking up with my bro. It doesn't mean I want to see it happen—or hear it either." He took a large bite, chewing as he glanced between us.

"I think it would be appropriate payback for what you and Tana have put us through repeatedly," Brittney said. She slipped her hand in mine, lacing our fingers together, and I felt a thrill course through me.

I couldn't help staring while she looked at me, and I forgot Brett was sitting there. Suddenly all I could see was Brittney—all I could feel was the way she was making my heart race—all I knew was how excited I was to see where our dating would take us, and I realized for the first time in a long while what I was feeling. Hope. I had hope for the future again. She'd restored that for me.

I leaned in and kissed her mouth. "Thank you."

She looked confused. "For what?"

"For everything." I left it at that as Brett grumbled beside us, but I wished I could show her what I meant. Something was changing inside me, and I knew she was the reason why.

"Pedal faster," I groaned as the droning sound of a low flying airplane came from overhead. I looked up, watching for a moment as the jet prepared for landing at Sky Harbor, then glanced toward Brittney. "You aren't doing your share, and the boat is going in circles."

"I'm trying," she growled, glaring as the ripples in the water of Tempe Town Lake swirled around our small craft, reflecting some of the newer high-rise buildings which had grown up around it. "Some of us aren't blessed with legs from the football gods. My flabby limbs don't have a quarter of the muscles yours do."

I snorted. "Well, then that's the hottest dang flab I've ever seen." I eyed her long legs from her lace up sandals to her short shorts. "They look pretty fit to me."

"They aren't as good as they used to be. Since I'm not doing cheer anymore, I've gotten out of shape."

"Don't kid yourself. You look perfect. There's not an

ounce of fat on you."

"That's because I sweat it all off the moment we got out of the car. Seriously, Chase. It's one hundred and fifteen degrees. Let's go lay on your couch under the ceiling fan in your nice air-conditioned apartment."

I looked at her flushed face. Her skin did kind of resemble a tomato. Maybe I should take her in.

I shook my head. "I can't do that."

"Why not?" She looked confused.

"Because the couch is dangerous territory. Since I've agreed to go slow with you, I don't think it's a wise place for us to be together."

"Oh for goodness sake. I didn't think you'd take me so literally." She grabbed my face between her hands and plastered a kiss to my lips.

I stiffened in surprise before devouring her mouth when she parted her lips, plunging my tongue inside to taste her. She sighed and slid her arms around my neck allowing the deepened kiss to continue for several moments. Everything stilled, and I could only hear our breathing and the sound of the traffic rushing by on the freeway before she suddenly pushed me away.

"Now will you take me home?" she asked, looking miserably flushed.

"It would be my pleasure, but it's still going to require you to pedal the boat correctly, or we'll never get off this lake."

She scowled at me. "Why did you bring me here?"

"I thought it was obvious," I replied, and she arched an eyebrow. "I've been trying to fill our time with activities which don't require our bodies to touch."

"Well, stop it. You have permission to touch me all you want if you'll help me escape this heat."

That painted a very tempting picture. "Deal, but you're gonna have to listen to my coaching."

"I'll do anything you say, just get this boat to

shore."

"Anything?" I grinned, my imagination going wild.

"Think with the right body part, Walker, and get us to shore."

I laughed and started giving her instructions, and we slowly made our way to the loading ramp. I grabbed her hand and helped her out, leading her to the car.

Once we were settled in my rental, I turned on the air-conditioning full blast and Brittney sighed in relief, holding her hands toward the vents, adjusting one to blow toward her face.

"That feels heavenly."

"It does," I agreed, unable to take my eyes off her. I couldn't help myself and leaned over to kiss her cheek.

She turned to me, smiling.

"I enjoyed the kiss on the water," I said.

"Well, yeah. I was under duress I'm afraid. I would've done anything to get out of there."

I laughed. "So you're saying you rescind your previous offer?"

"Did I offer something?" She gave a nervous laugh.

"Only that you'd allow me to touch you all I want."

"Hmmm." She bit her lip, and I kissed it.

There was no way I was taking no for answer. I'd been burning up, on fire for her over a week now as we "dated" every day. She'd made a deal. I was holding her to it. I reached past her, grabbing the seat lever and making her recline. She gave a short yelp of surprise, and I leaned against her, ravishing her mouth. It felt really good to have her under me as I explored her lips, running my hands on the smooth skin exposed by her bikini top.

"Chase," she mumbled against me, pushing me slightly. "We're in the middle of the parking lot in full sun. Anyone can see us."

"I don't care," I muttered, kissing her some more.

"Take me home," she breathed, and I reluctantly pulled away to start the car. She readjusted her seat, and we sped off down the road toward the apartments.

She started giggling.

"What?" I asked, casting a glance in her direction.

"Nothing." She was grinning.

"What?" I asked again. "You're starting to give me a complex."

"It's nothing. I was just beginning to wonder if I've unleashed a beast."

"Oh, I'm definitely beastin' when it comes to you doll."

Her eyes widened, and she giggled once again. "I'm a little nervous, I think."

I laughed as we stopped at a light. "You should be." I let my gaze wander over her before glancing into her eyes. She honestly did look a bit anxious. Good. I liked throwing her off balance.

After we parked, I opened her door and kissed her again. She shoved me away, though, and started running toward the apartment. "It's too hot!"

I chased after her, catching her on the stairs and turning her around to kiss me again. She kissed back hard, jumping to wrap her legs around my waist, and I carried her the rest of the way up, leaning her against the wall as I fumbled for the knob, not breaking our connection.

The blast of cool air hit us when the door opened, and she sighed again as I stepped inside kicking it shut behind us. I carried her toward the hall, propping her against the wall again, so I could open the bedroom.

"Wait! Stay right here," she mumbled, pointing to the air vent overhead which was blowing directly on us. I gave into her demand, losing myself in kissing first her mouth and then down her neck as she curved against me.

"Mmm, that feels so good," she said, her eyes closed, her face enraptured.

"What does?" I asked as I continued skimming my lips over her skin. "The air vent or me?"

"Yes," she replied, and I grinned.

A loud slamming noise caused as both to jump, and I looked to see Brett standing outside his room with a scowl. "I'm pretty sure procreating against a wall does not fall in the realm of taking it slow."

I leaned my head against Brittney's chest and sighed. The moment was gone, and she released her legs and slid to the floor.

"Way to kill the mood, bro," I grumbled.

He smiled. "It's my job as twin brother."

"Actually, my mood is fine," Brittney said as she reached for my hand. "Come on, Chase." She opened the door to my room, and I couldn't help flashing Brett a grin as she pulled me inside.

~Chapter Eighteen~

"What is it with you and hot activities?" Brittney asked as I handed her a canteen. She looked amazing in her form-fitting white t-shirt, and my gaze traveled to her cut off shorts, over her long, tan legs, down to her trendy hiking boots. She was totally casual today, wearing very little makeup, her hair pulled through the hole of her matching white ball cap which had the word CHEER written across it in blue letters.

"Maybe I just like making you sweat." I winked at her before glancing at the overcast sky. "Besides, it's not that bad today after the storm we got last night. It's lowered the temperature a good fifteen degrees."

She rolled her eyes. "Yeah, now it's only one hundred instead of a hundred and fifteen."

I laughed. "It's was only eighty-five this morning when I got up. Perfect hiking weather."

"Well, it's not eighty-five now," she replied. "You know it as well as I do."

"Maybe, but I'm betting it will still be a nice afternoon. Then again, we might get lucky and get sprinkled on while we're out. You realize this is going to be one of the last free Saturdays I have in months. I've always wanted to hike to Flat Iron and see the view of the valley below. I thought it might be kind of romantic to share with you."

She didn't look too convinced as she stared at the trail which led into the towering Superstition Mountains with its rigid, red cliff faces adorned with peaks and pinnacles.

"What are you worried about?" I asked, slinging the strap of my own canteen over my shoulder.

"Oh, I don't know . . . maybe that I'll be the person who ends up on the six o'clock news—you know, the stupid hiker that has to be rescued by helicopter."

I laughed. "What if I swear to protect you and keep that from happening?"

"You promise not to fall off a cliff or faint from heat stroke and leave us both stranded?"

"I promise. Scouts honor," I replied.

She snorted. "You were a Boy Scout?"

I grinned. "Would it make you feel better if I said yes?"

"Only if it's true." She gave me a narrowed squint.

"Hmmm. Let's get going then." I slipped my hat on before sliding a trim backpack on. Shutting the door to my truck, I activated the alarm and slid the keys into the pocket of my tan cargo shorts. I grabbed Britt by the hand, interlacing our fingers.

"You were never a scout were you?" She scowled.

"Don't you trust me?" I cast a sidelong glance at her. "I'm hurt by your lack of faith in me."

"Why won't you answer the question?"

"Fine," I responded with mock frustration as we left the parking lot, gravel crunching under our feet as we stepped onto the trail. "You win. I was never a Boy Scout, but I've been hiking, fishing, boating, camping—you name it. I've had lots of experience with roughing it out-of-doors. I swear I'll take care of you. You're in great physical shape. This will be a piece of cake I bet."

"I've heard lots of people say this was a difficult hike." She still seemed apprehensive.

"We will take it as slowly as we need to. We've got plenty of time. Just try to relax and enjoy it."

"Only if you promise me one thing."

"What's that?"

"You let me pick the next date."

I chuckled. "Deal."

She smiled then, and bumped me with her elbow. "There is one good thing about this."

"Tell me."

"I get to have you to myself for the entire day."

"That does sound awesome. We don't get nearly enough alone time, in my opinion. And it's only going to get worse once the games start."

"We'll have to make sure we have quality time if we can't have quantity time then."

"I'm all for that." My eyes darted about, studying the dirt trail ahead of us. There was a real possibility of coming across rattlesnakes this time of year. I wanted to keep my word and make sure Brittney was safe, but I was also leery of warning her about them. I worried she'd freak out and go running back to the truck.

"So how long is this hike?" she asked, staring up the gentle incline of the slope ahead.

"If we make it all the way up and back, it will be just under six miles." I pointed to a triangular area jutting from the side of the mountain. "See over there? That's where we're trying to get."

"That's high."

I nodded. "It's around a nine hundred foot change in elevation. Are you okay with it?" I decided to be nice and give her one last chance to ditch out. I didn't want her to feel forced. "I want you to have fun too."

"Don't worry. I will. I enjoy doing stuff with you. Let's rock this hike." She smiled and picked up her pace enough that she was dragging me along behind her. "Hurry slow poke. Sheesh."

"Oh, don't even." I poked her in the side, tickling her, and she let go of my hand and ran ahead.

"Britt, wait!" I chased after her, knowing she wasn't aware of the dangers that could be ahead. She didn't slow, and I hurried faster, grabbing her around the waist and yanking her against me. "Hold still and listen," I said, slightly winded from running uphill.

"What?" She was laughing and tried to squirm out of my embrace.

"I didn't tell you this because I didn't want you to worry, but we need to watch for snakes on the trail. They like to lie in the warm sun."

She stilled immediately. "Snakes? Like rattlesnakes?" She glanced around frantically.

"Any kind, but yes, those too. Pay attention where you step, and check around rocks we might stop to rest on, before you sit, okay?"

She nodded, biting at her lip as she continued scanning the area with a worried gesture.

I sighed. "Are you sure you don't want to go home? I don't think you're having a very good time."

She straightened her shoulders, showing her resolve. "No. I want to do this. I'll be fine. I'm glad you invited me. It tells me you think I'm up for the challenge."

"I do think it. You're in great shape already, and you said you wanted to work out. I thought it would be a cool experience."

She laced her hand in mine, and we started walking again. "It will be, I'm sure, but for future reference, when I speak of working out, I'm thinking air conditioned gym."

I laughed. "Point taken."

The view from the top was incredible, almost like we could see the curve of the earth as we stared over the flat metropolis which stretched beneath us until it met and blended with the gray sky on the horizon. The climb had been an intense workout, but it was worth it to get here and see the far reaching vista, a blend of desert mixed with splashes of green saguaros and tree tops, with Spanish tiled roofs. To the left of us, miniature looking vehicles moved along Highway Sixty, but from this height all we could hear was silence.

I stepped behind Britt and wrapped my arms around her waist, resting my chin on the top of her hat. "Gorgeous, isn't it?"

"It's breathtaking." She slid her palms over the backs of my hands. "Thank you for bringing me."

"Thanks for being willing to give it a try. I've loved every moment we've been together today."

"Me too." She continued stroking me softly, and I noticed we were swaying gently from side to side. "I wish we could see this at night. I bet it's magical when the city is lit up."

"That would be incredible. Maybe we can check into camping here someday. Then we could see it."

She giggled. "Are you trying to get me alone in a tent out in the middle of nowhere?"

I squeezed her tighter. "I suddenly find myself hard-pressed to think of anything I might enjoy better." My rampant imagination sprang eagerly to life.

She turned and wrapped her arms around my neck, popping up to place a soft kiss against my lips. "I can almost hear that mind of yours going a million miles a minutes."

I chuckled and kissed her again. "I have no idea what you're talking about."

"Uh huh. Sure you don't." She kissed me again. "Please tell me you've got something delicious in your backpack, because I'm starving."

"I brought energy bars, trail mix, and jerky." I released her so I could shrug it off.

"That sounds divine." She walked to a large rock, and after checking around it, sat down. A sudden breeze whipped her ponytail about, making her hair flip around her face. She turned to glance toward the valley below. "Where did that come from?"

"I don't know, but I'm not complaining. It feels great. You were right about the temperature. It's pretty humid today." I dug through my knapsack and handed her several food items. "Here you go. Take your pick. How's your canteen doing? I've got some extra bottles of water in here too."

She unscrewed the lid and checked inside. "I've still got about half."

I frowned. "You need to drink more. You're going to get dehydrated if you don't."

"I didn't want to drink too much. I've noticed there aren't many handy bathrooms."

"That's what bushes are for."

"That's easy for you to say. You're a guy. You can pee standing up. Knowing my luck I'd pick the bush that covered the entrance to a snake pit."

I shook my head. "Yeah, that'd be bad . . . I'd be forced to suck the poison out."

She blushed heavily. "You're incorrigible."

I couldn't help my grin. "So I've been told." I sat beside her, breaking open a bag of jerky and offering her some. She took a piece and started chewing, and I popped a piece between my lips before bending over the pack to dig out some water to refill her canteen.

"Um, Chase?"

I heard the concern in her voice and sat up. "Yeah?"

"What's that?" She pointed toward the horizon.

I followed her line of sight and felt a bit of dread creep over me. "Put your canteen on, Britt, and get up. We've got to go. We can't get caught in that." I looked at the giant dust storm billowing up like an enormous rolling cloud that reached thousands of feet into the air as it engulfed the surrounding area for miles. Even though it looked far away, it was monstrous and I knew there was no possible way we could get to the truck before it hit. "We need to climb those few feet back down the cliff face, and get to safer ground."

She didn't say a word, but quickly helped me gather our things and load them again. We hurried in the direction we'd come, trying to move as fast as possible. I was nervous. I'd seen the damage first hand these horrific monsoon storms could do. They often brought sections of the city to a complete standstill, snapping power lines and trees like matchsticks, knocking out the utilities of thousands, shutting down air traffic, even producing microbursts of tornado-like activity. If we got stuck here, no one would be able to help us until the storm passed. We were going to need to find a place with some cover.

Running down the trail was easy since it was steep, but we often had to move forward in a back and forth motion—like switchbacks—to slow our progress, so we didn't lose control. We didn't speak, gripping each other by the hand as we hurried along, watching our footing and occasionally glancing to check on the progress of the storm which was raging ever closer, swallowing everything in its path.

Despite the popularity of this trail, we hadn't seen another soul hiking today. We were in this alone . . . the two of us against Mother Nature.

We'd managed to make it about half a mile before I knew our time was up. The wind had increased significantly, pelting us with stinging grains of dirt. I paused, glancing around the terrain. "Over there, Britt. See that outcropping of rock with the low overhang? That's where we're heading."

I didn't wait for her to reply, and the two of us took off running. I said a silent prayer there wouldn't be any snakes taking refuge in the space as well.

"Lie on your side and slide under there!" I ordered

loudly over the roaring sound of the wind.

She moved quickly, and I stopped long enough to shrug my backpack off and toss it underneath before I scooted into the small space, my back facing the entrance.

"If the dust gets too bad, pull your shirt over your face to help filter the air, okay?"

She nodded, her eyes wide in the dim light.

I dug into my pocket for my cell phone, turning it on and checking for service. It had a couple of bars, so I dialed Brett's number. It went straight to message. "Brett, we're on the trail, stuck in the storm." I had to yell over the howling wind, the metallic taste of the dust settling into my mouth. "I think we're about half a mile down from the top—the route is marked on the map I left with you. We've taken cover in a crevice under a rock, and we're okay for now, but we're unable to keep going. I'm turning on my location services. If you don't hear from us again, send help. I've had my phone off all day, so I have a full charge. Call me when you get this." There was a crackling sound, and the line went dead. I quickly enabled the location setting and slid it into my pocket.

"I'm scared." I hardly heard her shaking voice over the sound of the wind whipping and whistling through the rocks of the narrow canyon.

I shifted the bag lower between us and pulled the upper portion of her body into the cradle of my arms. "Don't be afraid," I spoke next to her ear. "Think of this as part of the adventure." The light around us had quickly darkened and taken on a decidedly brownish hue. "We'll be okay. Brett will get the message, and I left a map with him of where we were going today. This is just a detour in our plans. Look at the bright side . . . it can't last forever, now can it?"

A bright flash, followed immediately by a loud crack

of thunder, made us both jump. I was suddenly very glad we were under this rock.

Brittney instinctively scooted back farther, moving the few extra inches until her back was pressed against the stone. Her fingers tightened around my neck, dragging me closer. "Get in as far as you can!"

I scooted closer, and we both flinched again at another flash and deafening crack.

"Those are hitting the ground," she said, as it rumbled beneath us.

I nodded. "I know. I can feel it."

"I can see them behind you. I'm terrified, Chase!"

I could feel her trembling. "Look at me. Don't watch the storm, focus on me." Her eyes were wide with fear, panicked, and I wished I could make her feel better somehow—take her mind off the dangerous situation we were in.

My mouth descended quickly to hers, and I felt her stiffen in surprise before she relaxed slightly. She returned my kisses almost frantically, her fingers digging into my scalp as she held me tightly, both her desire and fear jumbled together.

The distraction worked for both of us as I buried my face against her neck, kissing her there as well, my arm sliding down to her hip in an effort to bring her body closer to mine, but the backpack was in the way, and I groaned in frustration.

My mind faintly registered a change in the smell of the air, and I realized it had started raining. I kept kissing her as the sound of a torrential downpour now joined the rest of the storm's wild noises. I could feel the back of my shirt starting to get wet.

We were in big trouble. I'd seen the watermarks against the rocks in the area around us, and the odds of a flash flood were great. If that happened, we'd be stuck here, unable to cross several parts of the trail.

She pulled away, staring at me, concerned. "What's the matter, Chase?"

My phone buzzed against my leg. I quickly grabbed it from my pocket. "Brett?"

"Where are you, man? Are you okay?"

"It's pouring. I'm worried we're gonna be stuck here for the night." Brittney became rigid at my words, nervousness washing across her face. I stared at her as I continued talking to Brett. "The watershed runs right through here. There's no way we'll be able to get back down to the truck. We still have plenty of food and water to last us a while, but I don't know how long it'll be before we can safely cross the trails again. Check the news. See if they know how long the storm is supposed to last."

"I'll call you right back," Brett said, hanging up.

"We have to stay here all night?" Brittney asked.

"There's a good possibility of that. Hopefully the water will be down enough we can cross in the morning." I shifted, casting a glance over my shoulder and could see a steady stream tumbling its way through a lower section of the rock. "I don't want to risk getting caught in a flood area."

"Me either. I've seen on the news how quickly those can turn bad. Are we safe where we are?"

"I think so. We're a little higher than everything else." Another bright flash and loud boom rattled us.

"I don't like those," she whimpered.

"I know, me neither." I hugged her tighter, and she buried her head under my chin, nuzzling against my chest. My phone vibrated again, and I answered it.

"Hang in there, dude. I called 911. They're sending a rescue crew. I gave them your number. They're going to be calling and coordinating with you."

I was relieved. I'd face the humiliation of being rescued if it meant getting Brittney safely off this mountain. "Thanks, Brett. I'll call you when we get out of here."

"What's happening?" Brittney asked.

"He called 911. They're sending a rescue crew."

To my surprise she started laughing.

"What?"

"I told you we were going to end up on the six o'clock news."

I grinned. "I guess you did. I'll remember to pay more attention to you next time."

She held my face in her hands and smiled. "When it comes to hiking, Walker, I can promise you—there will be no next time."

I laughed and kissed her again.

Part Two

~Chapter Nineteen~

I threw the pass as hard as I could, smiling as the sold-out crowd shot to their feet when the receiver caught it and ran it in for a touchdown. I'd been in lots of football games, but nothing had prepared me for the sound of seventy thousand plus fans rising to their feet and screaming all at once.

"Touchdoooooooown! Sun Devils!" the announcer's voice boomed through the stadium. "That was a forty yard pass from number twenty-three, Walker, the freshman quarterback to the senior, Nelson. The score is now ASU Sun Devils 20, U of A Wildcats, 7."

The crowd roared again, and I couldn't help my grin. This was our biggest rival game here, in the home state, and we were rockin' it.

"Great pass, Walker," Coach Bell yelled, smacking me on the helmet with his clipboard. "Keep it up!"

"I will, Coach." I went to the water table and grabbed a bottle, squeezing some of the refreshing liquid in my mouth before removing my helmet and dousing some over me as well.

I glanced up into the stands, seeing Brittney and Tana sitting together in the special reserved section for wives and girlfriends. She waved at me and blew a kiss. I smiled at her before turning back to the field to watch the special teams do the point-after attempt and kick off.

Life was amazing. In the two months Brittney and I had been together, things had moved very quickly, and I found myself completely wound up in her. The ache in my heart for Nikki was still present, as it probably always would be, but it didn't torture me nearly as bad these days. I'd gone so far as to put her picture away in a drawer, only to come home from practice one night to find Brittney sitting on my bed staring at it before putting it back in its usual place. I'd given her a questioning look.

She shrugged. "I miss her, and you love her. I think it's important for her to be where you can see her still. She was a good part of your life."

My heart warmed at her generosity. "I love you too." It was the first time I'd said the words.

Her eyes widened, and a smile emblazoned across her face. "You do?"

I nodded, dropping my duffle bag and went to the bed and wrapped my arms around her. "I do."

She kissed my lips lightly, and there were tears in her eyes. "I love you too. I've been afraid to say it because I didn't want to put any undue pressure on you."

I stroked her hair away from her face and pecked her lips again. "You don't ever need to be afraid to tell me what you're feeling, Britt. I want to hear it all, but first you have to make a deal with me."

She looked confused. "What's that?"

"I want you to take a picture with me to go on my nightstand next to Nikki's picture."

"I'd love to do that. Maybe Tana can take one for us."

"Sounds great," I'd replied and started kissing her again.

I smiled to myself as I thought of the amazing picture of Britt and I in each other's arms now sitting next to Nikki's. I liked having the two pictures together. It was almost like Nikki was smiling about us.

The defense ran onto the field, setting up for the

Wildcat offense.

"What are you grinning about over here by yourself?" Brett's voice interrupted as he pounded my shoulder pad with a fist.

"Nothing. Happy, I guess. Things are going really good right now." I laughed. "I sound sappy."

"No you don't. You should feel good. How many guys can say they're da bomb starting quarterback for a four year college? You're dating the girl you wanted, your classes are going well, you've got your truck back, and you have the best roommate in the world. People would kill for your life, man."

"I'm just trying to be me."

"And it works for you. I think poor Matt is about to go into a fit of rage every time he sees you, he's so jealous."

I cast a glance down the line to where Matt was standing, glaring at me. "You're probably right, but it's his own fault. He was dating the perfect girl, and he cheated on her. He deserved to be ditched."

"He's still hanging around with Jared too, ever since he got kicked off the team. Both of them hate you. You know this right? I'd be careful, bro."

"I'm aware of it," I replied, turning my attention to the field once more. "I'm fairly certain they're the ones who smashed up my truck. I don't know how to prove it, though."

"It makes sense to me. I wonder if they're trying to goad you into a fight, so you'll get kicked off too."

"I have no idea, but I don't really care. I'm not gonna waste my time and energy thinking about them. I've got better things to do."

Brett groaned. "Please tell me when you say the word "do", you mean football and homework . . . *not* my sister."

I laughed loud, caught off guard.

His eyes narrowed. "What? No comment?"

The crowd cheered wildly as ASU intercepted the ball.

"Sorry, bro. No time to answer. Gotta go back to work." I headed onto the field leaving Brett grumbling under his breath behind me. It was time to finish this game.

"You were amazing tonight," Brittney said as we cuddled together on my bed.

"How's that possible? I haven't started yet."

She tried to shove me away, but I clenched her tighter. "In the game, silly."

I chuckled. "Oh, that. Yeah, I guess I did okay. The line did a good job of protecting me."

"Quit pushing the glory off on to others. You rocked, and you know it."

"If I was any good, it's because I knew you were watching. I can't put on a bad show for my girl, now can I?"

"You'd have been amazing whether or not I was in attendance. Chase Walker never does anything half way."

"Is that so? When did you become such an expert on me?" I kissed the side of her mouth.

"I've been studying . . . a lot, or haven't you noticed?" She kissed me back.

"Please continue your studying. I quite enjoy it—or perhaps I should be the one studying." I rolled her over so she was underneath me.

"You mean you haven't been?" Her white-blonde hair was spread over my pillow.

"No—not studying—memorizing." I lowered my mouth to hers, dipping my tongue between her plump lips, enjoying the intimate taste of her.

She wrapped her arms around my neck, followed by

hooking her legs around my waist, and I groaned against her as she pulled away slightly.

"You're my prisoner," she whispered. "Now you can't escape."

"I was already your prisoner, and I never want to escape." I kissed her again, slow, languid, and deep. She sighed heavily.

"What's the matter?" I asked.

"Nothing. I like the way you kiss. Keep doing it."

I did as she asked.

"Where did you learn to kiss like this?"

"God given talent," I muttered against her skin as I slid down her neck.

She slapped my shoulder. "I'm serious."

I locked eyes with her. "Do you really want to know? I'm not sure you do."

"I wouldn't have asked if I didn't want to know."

I sighed, seeing how this conversation could turn bad in a hurry. "I've made out with lots and lots of girls." I watched her closely for her reaction.

"And what makes me different from those girls?" She looked nervous.

"I'm in love with you. These kisses mean something . . . they're not simply for gratification."

"How many others were you in love with?"

I sighed, moving off her to sit up. "Only one, and you know all about her. Why the sudden questions?"

She shrugged and sat up next to me. "I'm not sure, but I honestly want to know." She fiddled with her shorts before running her hand over the blanket.

"Is something wrong?" I asked.

She shook her head. "No. Not really."

"Britt, talk to me. I can't read your mind. You have to tell me what's going on in that head of yours."

She glanced toward Nikki's picture, silent for several moments, and I waited for her to speak.

"I feel kinda like I won you by default sometimes. I mean, I know you love me, but if Nikki were here, let's face it—you and I would've never happened. I would've broken up with Matt, and then what? Been lonely? Would I have watched you and Nikki together and been jealous? I feel like the second choice. I don't want to feel that way, but I do. If she were to reappear right now, you'd go right back to her, wouldn't you?"

Damn, damn, damn. I really did not need this right now. I didn't have a clue how to answer her. I ran my hand over my head. "Britt, I don't know why things happen the way they do, but I can promise you—you were never my second choice."

She wrinkled her brow in confusion. "What do you mean? I don't understand."

"I mean you were the first girl who caught my attention when I moved to Silver Creek. You sat there in class giving me these shy smiles. I thought you were hot, and I would've hit on you, but Matt was hanging all over you—clearly marking you as his territory. I was new and didn't want to push it. I figured there were other fish in the sea. Then I saw Nikki, and she was beautiful too—it progressed from there. Who knows why things happen the way they do? If you hadn't been with Matt, it might have been you I went after. We could've dated and then Nikki wouldn't have been coming to meet me at all. Maybe she would still be alive."

"Oh, Chase . . . ," she began, resting her hand on my arm.

"No. Stop, okay? If there's one thing I've learned, it's that what you said is true—playing the "what if" game won't get you anywhere. It only creates more hurt. Can I say what I'd do if Nikki walked in here right this moment? No. I can't. Why? Because even though I'd be thrilled to see her, I'd be devastated too. I'd be in love with two amazing girls and know I'd end up hurting one of them by choosing the other. So, let's do this instead. Let the past lie, Britt, there's no possibility of a future for it. I don't know why fate let things play out the way they did, but you're my here and now. It's all that matters to me. Yes, tragedy brought us together, but I can't imagine my life without you. Don't ever think you're here by default. I love you."

Her chin trembled as she fought back tears. "I'm sorry. I don't mean to be weird about things. It's been weighing heavily on my mind. I think deep down I'm . . . jealous of her. I don't want to be because I love her too. She was one of my best friends. But I can't help thinking if she were still alive, it would be her here in my place, and you'd be super happy. It's hard for me to get over."

"I understand what you're saying, but I'm telling you it doesn't matter. You're my future. You and I will do stuff together I only dreamed about with Nikki. You—you're the one those things will happen with. You're the reality. Don't doubt my feelings for you. Nikki—she was there for me when I needed her the most. She helped to shape and change me into the guy who'd fall in love with you. I'm better because of it, and you're getting a better me because of it too." I was frustrated. I didn't know how to properly express what I was feeling—I only knew I was desperate for her to know I loved her—I mean really, truly loved her.

"I liked you from the first moment, Chase. I'm glad Nikki helped you with stuff, but I thought you were pretty awesome to begin with."

"You did?"

"I did. I watched how you went after her. You did the most romantic things—and you respected her too. Matt was never that way with me. He'd blame me for things he did wrong, like when he got pulled over for speeding one day. He said it was my fault for distracting him. If he didn't like someone, then he didn't want me to talk to them either. He hated when I was around you." She sighed heavily. "I wasted so much time with him—time that could've been spent with you if I'd been brave enough to walk away."

"Well, guess what? You're not with that jerk anymore, and I'm always willing to shower you with romantic things." I smiled, placing my hand over hers.

"I know. You have been already. I guess I'm only wishing I'd been lucky enough to find you sooner."

"Better late than never, right?"

She looked up, and a soft smile played on her lips. "Better late than never. Now kiss me, Walker," she ordered, so I did.

~Chapter Twenty~

I tried not to do the jello-neck-head-bob during my required Sociology class, but it was proving dang near impossible. Who thought up these stupid curriculums anyway? There was a cute brunette sitting to my left who kept trying to catch my attention during the lecture, and I was doing my best to avoid eye contact with her.

My mom had been right. Being the quarterback at a big university made the girls come crawling out of the woodwork. I remembered the days when I used to be nervous about asking girls on a date, and it made me chuckle. I had to practically beat them off with a stick now. The old me would've loved hanging and partying it up with a different girl every night, but that was before Nikki, and now Brittney. I was crazy about her, and no one else could compare.

Not that I was getting to spend any time with her. I was in these dumb classes all day, practice until after dark, then games on the weekends—which were away a lot, so I was traveling too. The only time we ever got to spend together was nights and Sundays. We fell asleep together almost every evening, piled under a mountain of homework we were trying to finish. I'd often come home from trips to find her curled up on my couch or bed with textbooks all over her. I'd carefully remove them so I wouldn't wake her before lying down and wrapping my arms around her. I missed her.

There didn't seem to be an end in sight, either. It was only October, and the season would run through

January. We needed a break soon, and I'd begun to formulate a plan to surprise her with on Sunday.

I didn't realize I'd dozed off until I heard the teacher call my name, and a bunch of the students snickered around me. I noticed the stern expression on her face as she stared at me over the top of her glasses.

"If you want to continue playing football, Mr. Walker, I suggest you start paying attention in class." This was the second part of the problem—being the quarterback also meant all the teachers knew who I was too. They might not know who ninety-nine percent of the student body was, but people tended to remember the name of the kid whose face was on television and in the sports section of the newspaper frequently.

"Sorry Mrs. Miller," I said politely, staring down at her from where I sat several rows up in the amphitheater styled seating. "It's been a long week."

"Well, it's time to pull your priorities together."

My priorities don't include your class, I thought. "Yes, ma'am." I said what she wanted to hear so she'd get off my case.

"You don't want to get behind anymore than you are. Otherwise you won't be eligible to play. You might want to consider getting a tutor if you can't keep up with things." She returned her attention to the blackboard, and I had to bite my tongue to keep from blurting that my grade in her class was several points above eligibility range, despite the one assignment I'd neglected to turn in. I was pissed she'd singled me out to reprimand in front of the whole class.

"I'd be happy to help tutor you," the brunette to my left whispered, and I had to acknowledge her.

"Thanks," I said, smiling nicely. "I already have a tutor, though."

"Oh." She looked disappointed before she stopped to scribble something on a piece of paper and hand it to me. "Well, if it doesn't work out, here's my number. Feel free to give a call anytime." She smiled widely, and I took it, reading what she'd written.

"Thanks again . . . Lexie," I replied, glancing at her name. "Oh, I see you put your dorm room number here too." Talk about obvious. I had to stop myself from rolling my eyes.

"Yeah." She tossed her hair behind her shoulder, as she cast a seductive glance over me. "In case you want to . . . study at my place."

"Super. You're awesome. I'll be sure to have my girlfriend file this for me." I stared pointedly at her, and she had the decency to keep her mouth shut and turn away. The class time was up, saving me from any further awkward conversations, so I gathered my books and headed toward the door, depositing Lexie's number in the wastepaper basket on the way past.

I checked my phone and saw I had a message from Brittney. I dialed my voicemail and listened.

"Hey," Brett said joining me from his class down the hall. "Ready for lunch?"

"Yeah. We need to run to the store for Britt, though. She's stuck at work and can't take a break."

"Let's go then. We can pick up whatever she needs on the way."

While I was thrilled to have a girlfriend who felt like she could talk to me about anything, I found myself very frustrated and amazed. I was confident no one would think I was standing in this section of the store for my own benefit, but I honestly would've given my right arm to be anywhere else in the world than here.

"Grab a box and let's go," Brett said, looking around nervously.

"Which one? There's like a thousand of them."

"I don't know. Aren't they all the same? Did she ask

for something specific when she called?"

"No. She just said tampons. You're her brother, dammit. Didn't you pay attention to these kinds of things?"

"Oh, hell no. I'd rather pluck my own eyeballs out than be around a woman on her period."

"What kind does Tana use?"

"Did you not hear my last statement?"

A woman pushed her cart between us and the massive wall of feminine hygiene products. She grabbed a box and placed it in her cart.

"Are those the good kind?" Brett blurted, and I elbowed him in the ribs, mortified.

The woman gave us a strange stare, like we were some kind of deviants.

"My girlfriend sent me to pick some up for her," I offered lamely before she called security.

"Oh!" She smiled as if everything made sense now. "Well, what size does she like?"

"There's a size?" Brett asked, dumbfounded.

"Well, yes. It helps to know how heavy her—"

"Never mind," I said snatching a random box off the shelf. "This box looks good. Thanks for your help."

I practically ran from the aisle before turning to Brett who was following close behind. "Here, you carry these." I held the box toward him.

"You couldn't pay me enough to carry those." He stepped backward as if I were holding a culture dish carrying the black plague inside.

"It's for *your* sister," I said shoving the box in his direction.

"She's *your* girlfriend, and she asked *you* to get them. Besides, how do you know this isn't some sick, twisted, female test? You won't pass if I show up with them."

I tucked the tampons under my arm with a growl

and headed toward the register.

"It's not like people are gonna think they're yours," Brett added with a laugh.

"Shit!" I uttered the curse as several guys from the team stepped from an aisle a few feet ahead of us. I quickly tossed the box toward Brett, who reflexively caught it, stunned.

"Hey dudes! Wassup!" Garret Hunt, one of the D-linemen called coming to give me high five, followed by the others.

"Nothin' much. Just pickin' up some stuff for Brett's period." I gestured to him with my thumb, and he glanced down at the item in his hand. "It's that time of the month."

Brett glared at me. "You are so dead."

I laughed. "He's a little moody too, so take it easy on him at practice today, okay?"

"No problem," Garret said with a grin, clapping Brett on the shoulder. "Hang in there, man. It'll pass."

The guys chuckled and continued on their way. "Catch ya later."

"Sure thing," I replied, moving toward the registers again. "You coming?" I asked Brett who was still fuming in the aisle.

"No. I'm thinking of ways to kill you."

"Ah, come on. It wasn't that bad."

"Mmhmm." He pursed his lips.

Later that evening, we walked into practice, and my eyes widened when I saw Brett's locker covered in pads, tampons, and boxes of Midol. Garret and the rest of the guys were standing around waiting for him and started laughing when they saw us. I couldn't help it—I laughed too.

Brett leaned close and whispered in my ear. "Man, you better *pray* I take the Midol because you're gonna need it!"

"Don't blame me! I didn't do it." I held my hands up and backed away innocently.

"You're just as guilty of doing it as if you'd taped the stuff up there yourself. If you'd have kept the stupid box, it would be *your* locker that looks like this."

"That's right. See, you took one for the team. I have a rep to protect. The QB can't be some tampon wearing fool." I headed toward my locker.

"Hey! Are you calling me a tampon wearing fool?"

"Would I do that?" I asked, tossing a grin over my shoulder.

"Yes. I do believe you would." He was glaring, and I couldn't help laughing harder.

"We got you a heating pad too, man," Garret said handing Brett a box as he approached. "I think you'll find it really helps those cramps."

Brett glowered at me and mouthed the word, DEAD. I couldn't stop snickering. I'd need to watch my back. He would definitely be looking for payback.

"Walker! I need to see you in my office!" Coach Bell's voice boomed through the space, interrupting Brett's and my banter.

I turned to head in that direction, giving Garret a high five as I passed. "Good job, bro. That's some friggin' funny stuff right there."

"I aim to please," Garret replied with a grin.

Coach gestured for me to take a seat. I did so, and he shut the door behind me, closing the blinds to the interior window of the locker room as well.

That wasn't a good sign. I was immediately on my guard.

"Is something wrong, Coach?"

He walked around his desk and sat down, leaning his arms on it as he stared at me. "Is there anything you want to tell me, son? You know if you're struggling with things, you can talk to me. I'll always listen to what you have to say and help any way I can."

I stared at him for a moment, completely befuddled as to what he was referring to. "Can you be more specific, because I truly have no idea what you're talking about."

He sighed deeply and picked up a piece of paper folded in front of him. "This was slipped under my door when I came in today."

I opened it, reading the typed message.

Your starting quarterback is on drugs. Check his locker.

I calmly tossed the paper back onto his desk. "I'm not on drugs. Feel free to check my things."

"I already did. I had security come do a legal search."

"Then you know it's not true."

He opened his drawer and lifted two bags, one contained marijuana and another pills. "We found these in your locker."

My heart sank, and my vision spun from shock. "Someone is setting me up, Coach. I've used in the past, yes, but I've been in addiction therapy to get past it. I've been clean ever since."

"How long ago was that?"

I thought back to Nikki's death and reading her journal, which had triggered my decision to get help. "It's been more than a year now since the last time I had any alcohol. Even longer than that for the dope."

He pondered this as he prodded the items on his desk. "If you're telling the truth, then I want you to submit to a random drug test right now. School policy dictates I suspend you from the team until your name is cleared. I'll do my best to keep this under wraps. We definitely don't want the press getting ahold of this."

"What about practice today? And the game

tomorrow?"

"As of right now, you're out sick. The lab is closed for the weekend, so they won't be doing the test until Monday. I'm thinking that afternoon will be the earliest we'll have results back—maybe even Tuesday morning."

"Are you serious?" I was fuming angry, pushing back my chair to stand. "You're honestly telling me I can't play because some asshole set me up? Anyone could've watched and got my combination. It's not like I hide it or anything." I took my cap off and ran a hand through my hair. "This will affect my stats. It's ridiculous!"

"The rules are rules, Chase. I don't want to do this either. My hands are tied. I want to believe you're telling me the truth, but I have to do things by the book. It can't appear as if I'm trying to protect you." He honestly looked apologetic.

"I *am* telling the truth." I was so angry I wanted to spit nails. Someone on *my* team was doing this to me.

"Then if that's the case, go into the restroom there and fill one of the collection cups on the counter." He gestured toward the private bathroom attached to his office. "After that, go home, and enjoy your weekend off. Sleep, watch movies, do whatever you want. Hopefully, I'll have good news for you on Monday."

"I have a date planned at the State Fair on Sunday with my girlfriend. Can I still do that? I've hardly seen her, and she got the day off work to be with me." I was boiling mad as I headed toward the bathroom.

He shrugged. "I don't see why not. Maybe you end up having some food poisoning?"

I shut the door, going over to pick up one of the sterile cups. When I found the dickwad who did this, there was gonna be hell to pay.

~Chapter Twenty-One~

"And the Sun Devils can't seem to make it work against the Huskies today. They're definitely missing Walker's passing game. Brubaker was brought up to play quarterback and is absolutely unable to connect with any of his receivers, coming at two for ten now," the television broadcaster stated.

"That's right, Hudson. Even the line seems to be faltering today, unable to get it together. It's almost like they've lost their confidence. What a day for Chase Walker to be sick with a case of food poisoning. It doesn't look good for ASU," the color commentator added.

I pointed the remote and clicked it off, slouching farther down against my couch. I couldn't stand to watch anymore.

"It serves them right," Brittney grumbled as she snuggled against me.

"What do you mean?" I asked.

"Someone on the team is setting you up. I don't know if they're after your position, or they want you gone, but they deserve to lose if that's the way they're gonna be."

"I'm pretty good friends with most of the guys on the team, Britt. They're good people. They don't deserve to lose."

She sighed. "I'm sorry. I know. I'm just kinda bitter. Your coach should've believed you."

"I think he does. He has set rules to follow, though. If he doesn't do things by the book, it'll look like a cover up on our part and could end badly. He's doing the right thing."

"Well, it still sucks." She wrapped her arm around my waist and hugged me tighter.

"I agree. Maybe you should do something to help me take my mind off it." I grinned, winking when she looked up.

"For a guy who's missing a big game, you don't seem very broken hearted."

"How can I be when it means I get to spend a whole extra day in your arms?" I kissed the top of her head. "I've missed you."

She smiled. "I've missed you too. Things have been crazy lately."

"They have been, but it'll be worth it."

"Hey, did you see the stack of mail I brought up for you? There was a big envelope from the school. Are you expecting something?"

"No, I don't think so. Where'd you put it?"

"It's here on the counter." She stood and walked around the corner briefly before reappearing, several items in her hands.

I took them from her, sorting the bills to the side before looking at the large manila envelope. I tore it open and peered inside.

"What is it?" she asked.

I shrugged. "It looks like more letters." I leaned forward and dumped the contents onto the coffee table. They were all addressed to the athletic department under my name. A piece of paper fell on the top, and I picked it up.

Fan mail for Chase Walker, it read. I started laughing.

"What does it say?" Brittney asked leaning over.

"Apparently, it's fan mail the school's received for me."

She giggled. "You have fans?"

I grinned. "Or haters."

"No way. No one could hate my Chase. I want to look at them with you."

"Okay." This was such a surreal feeling. I never imagined receiving anything like this. I grabbed one off the top of the pile and opened it, wondering what I'd find.

"Read it aloud," Britt said.

"Dear Chase. You don't know me, but I'm a sophomore at ASU. I come to watch all your home games, and I think you're the best quarterback we've ever had. I saw you take your helmet off on the jumbotron last time, while you were standing on the sidelines, and HOLY COW! You are HAWT!"

Brittney groaned and slumped back into the seat. "Great, fan letters from girls. I don't think I want to hear anymore."

I couldn't help chuckling as I continued. "I'd really love to meet you sometime. Here's my number, and you can find me on Facebook too. Hope to hear from you sometime soon!"

I glanced down to the bottom of the page where her number was written with a little smiley face on it.

"So are you gonna call this girl or what?"

I smiled, leaning to place a kiss against her mouth. "You should know better than to ask me that. My heart belongs to you."

That seemed to appease her because she grabbed another letter and handed it to me. "Your *fans* await. I swear these better not all be from girls."

This one was too, though she didn't try to give me her number. She told me how much she enjoyed watching me play, and it was a bonus that looking at me was fun as well. She closed by wishing me luck for the rest of the season. Brittney was rolling her eyes by the time I was through, but she handed me another.

We read one by one, sorting them into different piles. There was the "I want to date you" pile, which ironically wasn't all girls but a couple guys as well. That shocked me—I'd never had a dude hit on me before, and I didn't have the slightest clue how to handle it. There were amazingly sweet letters from younger kids. Some of them were from a class project a teacher organized, thanking me for being a good player and representing the state. Others were from local people who were fans of the game, wishing me good luck. All in all, there were thirty-five letters.

"This has been an interesting experience," I said as I relaxed against the couch.

Britt nestled against me again. "I know! You have fans! I still don't know if I like it."

"Well, you don't have to worry about the girls . . . or the guys for that matter. I would like to answer the kids, though." I sighed, feeling frustrated.

"What's the matter?"

"Nothing, really. I was thinking about this bogus drug charge. If it were leaked, it could do a lot to damage my reputation. It's not something I've ever worried about, but I guess I never realized how much younger kids look up to me. I never thought I'd be someone who was an example. It makes everything seem so much heavier. If I end up in the papers, suspended for possible drug use, those kids would feel let down. I don't want to disappoint people."

"You haven't disappointed anyone. You didn't do anything wrong." She stroked my cheek in a soothing manner.

"I know that, and you know that, but even when my name is cleared there will always be suspicion of did he or didn't he? I really don't want this to get leaked."

"Who would do that? I'm sure the team wants you

to have a good reputation."

"Someone doesn't. That person set me up."

"Any ideas who it might be?"

"Yep." I was hesitant to say. I knew she wouldn't like it. "I think it's Matt."

She was quiet, lowering her hand from my face to my stomach. "Why?"

"It's no secret we've never gotten along. He's hated me since the first time I laid eyes on you and flirted with you. He was best friends with Nikki's ex. I was also in an argument with one of his buddies on the team who tried to throw a punch at me and was kicked off as a result. Now we're dating after he found us together the morning you broke up with him. He knows he'll get kicked off the team if he tries to fight, so I think he's trying to come at me from a different angle or goad me into hitting him, so I'll get axed too. I'm not saying I'm great friends with every single guy on the team, but I think we all get along pretty passably. He's the only one I think who'd have it in for me."

"Why haven't you told me about this stuff before?" she asked, and I could tell she was upset about it by the way she pressed her lips together.

I shrugged. "It didn't seem important I guess."

"If someone's causing you problems, then it's important. You think he's the one who vandalized your truck up too, don't you."

"Either him or Jared, the guy who got kicked off. It could be the two of them together even. There was a lot of damage done."

She sat up and ran her fingers through her gorgeous hair in a frustrated gesture. "Is there anyone else who's mad at you I should know about?"
I shook my head. "I don't think so. Maybe Jennifer."

"Jennifer?"

"Yeah. She wasn't too thrilled with me when I told

her I was only making out with her because she reminded me of my dead girlfriend."

"Wow. No wonder she won't ever give me the time of day anymore. I tried to talk to her when I decided to date you, and she gave me the brush off. That was a little harsh don't you think?"

"I wasn't trying to be mean—she wouldn't listen, though. She kept trying to tell me all the reasons why we could work. I got tired of beating around the bush, so I laid it out straight for her. She got pretty angry with me after that—as you saw."

"Hmmm. Well, I still can't see her taking a bat to your truck."

"Me neither. I'm telling you—it's Matt. He's the only one of the three with access to the locker room. I really wish he'd have picked a different college team to walk onto. I thought for sure he'd go to school with Jeremy, since they were tight."

"He wanted to be where I was."

"Well, if he wanted to be by you so badly, he shouldn't have been chasing around with some ho."

She slapped me on the arm. "Don't call girls hos!"

I flinched away with a grin. "If the shoe fits . . . ," I said letting the sentence trail off.

"Keep it up, Walker, and I'm out the door."

"Oh, I can definitely keep it up," I said grabbing her and tossing her back on the couch, pinning her there. "Besides, do you really want to leave when we both have our places to ourselves for the first time in forever?" I lightly kissed her lips and she smiled.

"You're so bad."

"I've tried to warn you. But you keep telling me how good I am." I chuckled at the double meaning, and she sighed.

"You *are* good too." She pulled my face back to hers, and I melted into her embrace. I loved being in her arms—loved the way she made me feel. I thought this kind of relationship was lost to me forever. True, it was different from what I had with Nikki but wonderful still the same, perfect in its own right. It surprised me. I'd thought my life was finished when I'd lost Nikki. I didn't think I'd ever connect with anyone like this again. Brittney felt good—she felt right—maybe it was because we were friends first, but there was something . . . something different which made this feel unique. I couldn't quite put my finger on it, but I was looking forward to figuring it out.

My tongue dipped into her mouth, meeting hers, and I reveled in the taste. Everything about her flooded my senses; her light flowery scent—the way her skin felt like silk as I ran my fingers over it—the way she moved against me, causing me to feel so heated it was as if fire ran through my veins. I had to keep opening my eyes, because I couldn't get enough of the passionate expression on her face, and I loved knowing I was the one putting it there.

I kissed her hard, devouring her lips, pulling away as I teased at the bottom one with my teeth before moving to her neck, placing delicious nips all the way to her collarbone. Sweet little sounds escaped her as I trailed my way back up with the tip of my tongue, lightly latching onto her earlobe, and I felt her nails claw into me.

"You like this?" I asked, and I blew my heated breath against her.

"Yes," she huffed. "Please don't stop."

I grinned. "I never had any intention of doing that, but you need to relax. You keep tensing your muscles."

She laughed, quickly pecking my lips. "It's a natural reaction. It tickles, plus I have a knot it my shoulder from carrying trays at work."

"Well, we can't have that now, can we?" I got up

and extended my hand. "Come here."

She slipped hers into mine, and I pulled her into my room, guiding her to the bed. "Lay down on your stomach," I instructed, and she gave me a strange look before she did as I asked.

"What are you doing?" she questioned, turning her head, so she could see me.

I climbed onto the bed, straddling her, and leaned forward next to her ear. "Just relax, close your eyes and trust me," I whispered. As soon as she did, I gathered her long blonde hair and twisted it beside her head. Her breath caught when I slipped my fingers under her tank top and bra strap, exposing her bare shoulder as I pulled them off to the side.

Her skin was golden and smooth, and I couldn't help myself, I had to place a kiss there before I started to massage. She gave a small groan of pleasure, and liquid heat shot straight to my center. This girl had no clue how much she turned me on.

"Oh my gosh, Chase! You have no idea how good this feels."

I muttered some unintelligible reply, my mind immediately concocting a different scenario for which she could use those words. I let it play for a moment before slipping her clothing off the other shoulder and repeating the same actions there.

More sweet noises left her, and all I could think was how good her skin felt in my hands. I worked back and forth between the two spots before pushing her shirt down farther, so I could reach her shoulder blades. I felt her relaxing more and more, the longer I rubbed, which was funny to me, because I was only winding tighter and tighter.

I skimmed along the small of her back, lifting the hem of her shirt and pushing it up toward the middle. She flinched a bit as I lightly traced over her skin, and suddenly I couldn't take it any longer. I readjusted my position, replacing my fingers with my lips, and I heard her sharp intake of breath.

"You're killing me, Britt," I said so softly I wasn't sure if she could hear me. "I can't stop tasting you." My tongue dipped into one of the dimples of her back, just above her shorts, before continuing my path upward across her spine.

Her breathing increased as my warm breath brushed the back of her neck, and I didn't fail to notice the goose bumps that flared over her skin. I continued to feather my lips across her, lightly trailing my fingers up her side.

"Chase," she said in a slow exhale. "Let me roll over."

I chuckled seductively. "What if I don't wanna?" I could see part of her smile.

"I want to massage you now—you know, return the favor."

Oh, hell yes! I thought with glee. "Sounds fun," I said aloud, slipping to the side and laying on my back as if I was in total control, which was fine until she straddled me.

I couldn't help my obvious groan.

She grinned in conquering delight as she made a show of cracking her knuckles loudly. "Where should I start?"

"Here," I replied reaching my hands up and dragging her lips back to mine.

~Chapter Twenty-Two~

It was amazing how a few key smells could bring one's childhood rushing back from the dark recesses of the mind. I strolled hand in hand with Brittney as we walked down the midway behind Brett and Tana who were doing the same. We weaved through the throngs of people who were gawking at the spectacle before us, trying to decide how they'd throw their money away tonight.

I hadn't been to the State Fair in years, but everything was still situated the same way. Delicious smells floated in the air, the scents of deep fried food, buttered popcorn, and cotton candy—both sweet and greasy concoctions which were in no way healthy, but made my taste buds water just the same. Bright lights of every color flashed and spun as Carnies hocked their games and wares, or tried to get us to try their rides.

"What do you wanna do first?" I asked Brittney. Her face lit up like a kid in a candy shop as she watched several people scream in terror on a towering free fall ride.

"That makes me sick just watching it!" she exclaimed before covering her mouth and placing a hand against her stomach. "We should do it!"

I chuckled. "I can't believe you've never been to the fair before. My parents used to take me almost every year when I was younger."

"We lived too far away to make a special trip, and school was always going on." She pointed down a path which branched off the main one. "Look at those giant pillow pets! Oh my gosh! That would be so cool on my bed! I want you to win me one of those!" Her eyes continued to dart around. "Ooooh! Look how tall the Ferris Wheel is! Please, can we ride on it? I bet we can see the whole city from the top!

A pungent, musky odor briefly breezed past us, and we wrinkled our noses.

"Are there animals here too?" Brittney asked.

I nodded. "Lot's of people bring their livestock to show and sell. And there's a petting zoo too."

"A petting zoo! Let's go pet animals!" She clapped her hands together in delight.

"What do you need animals for?" Brett asked, rolling his eyes at her rabid excitement. "You've got one right beside you. Pet him. I'm sure he'd enjoy it."

I chuckled. "I'm not gonna lie—I'd *greatly* enjoy it." I grinned at Brittney as I hooked my arm around her neck and dragged her in close for a kiss, remembering the last time she'd had her hands on me.

She smiled against my mouth. "You're such a dork."

"Maybe, but it doesn't matter, because you love me anyway."

"I do. No doubt about it." She kissed me again.

"Enough already," Brett moaned. "We can't take anymore public displays of affection."

"When you and Tana stop, then we will stop too," Brittney countered, poking her tongue at him.

"The heck we will!" I protested. "I don't ever plan on stopping."

"You're such a guy, Chase." Tana laughed, glancing back at me. "Always thinking with . . . well, you know."

"Nothing wrong with that. It's how I'm engineered to think."

Brittney snickered and grabbed my hand, dragging me toward the Ferris Wheel. "Come on, Mr. Engineer. I think it's time for a ride."

I snorted as I glanced over her form. "Mmm. So do I." I winked, and she continued to giggle.

"Stop it."

"I can't."

"Why not?"

I shrugged. "I just can't."

"Can't or won't?"

I pondered this for a few seconds as she continued to pull me down the walkway. "Maybe some of both."

"That's not even possible!"

"Sure it is! I won't stop because I can't."

She paused, narrowing her eyes. "And why can't you exactly?"

I gathered her close, and she rested her hands lightly against my chest. "I can't because I don't ever want to stop telling you how you make me feel."

Her breath came out in a soft rush. "Oh, and how is that?"

"Alive. You make every part of me feel alive. It's the first time in a long time."

Tears welled in her eyes, and she popped up on her tiptoes. "I love you, Chase Walker," she whispered before pressing her lips to mine. I embraced her tighter as she slid her arms around my neck, kissing her fully and deeply for anyone around to see. But I didn't care. I loved her. She stepped away and slipped her hand back in mine, leading me through the loud, swirling, flashing, mayhem toward the ride.

Soon we were safely onboard and rising into the air. The lights and sounds of the fair dipped away beneath us, and we made our way upward . . . the twinkling yellow glow of Phoenix spread flat in the distance around us.

"Isn't it beautiful?" Britt said, snuggling closer.

"It is," I replied, sweeping her long hair to the side and bending to kiss her neck. She arched her head, releasing a small sound as I continued to brush over her skin, my tongue darting here and there to taste.

"Chase."

"Hmm?"

"People can see us."

I looked around, noticing the curious stares of those in the carts next to us. "Yep, they can." I reverted to kissing her neck.

"Can I tell you something?" She placed her hand on my knee and squeezed, causing me to pause.

"You know you can tell me anything."

She seemed anxious. "I never expected things to be so easy with you."

I smiled. "That's good right?"

"Yes—but also a little scary. We said we were going to take things slow."

I was worried now. "That was months ago, Britt. What are you saying? Is it too much?"

I was feeling a bit panicked, and I shifted in my seat causing the cart to sway abruptly. Brittney squealed, and grabbed onto my arm.

"Don't do that again!" I could tell she was terrified, and I wrapped my arm around her shoulders, hoping it would help her feel steadier.

"Then tell me what's going on?"

"Nothing's going on!" She sighed in frustration. "I'm not saying things right. All I meant was our relationship is going really fast, and I wondered what it means for us. Where do we go from here?"

Every muscle in my body relaxed, and I tried to calm my heart rate down. "Do we have to know where we're going, or can we let it happen naturally?"

"I want things to be natural, I'm just curious about the future. Where will we be a year from now, or two years? What if you get drafted to the NFL or something? What happens with us then?"

"Is that what you're worried about? That I'll move somewhere else and leave you?"

"It's a legitimate question." Her brow furrowed as if she were in serious thought.

"Where do you want to be if that happens, Brittney? Be honest. What do you want me to do if something like that comes up? Do you want me to turn it down?"

"No," she replied emphatically, looking down to toy with the hem of her shirt for a moment. I could tell she was nervous when she looked up at me. "I want you to take me with you."

I felt relieved. "Good, because if you didn't come with me, I wouldn't leave." I brushed my knuckles against her chin. "Quit worrying about this. You aren't some flash-in-the-pan rebound relationship. I want you. For real."

"But what if—"

"Shhhh," I interrupted, placing my finger over her lips to silence her. "There will be no playing the 'what if' game tonight. I love you—you love me—that's all either of us need to know right now. Okay?"

She nodded again. I wasn't actually sure if it was a nod of agreement or acquiescence, but she didn't try to stop me when I kissed her for the rest of the ride.

I handed the vendor my ticket card, and he scanned it before laying three baseballs in front of me. "You know these games are rigged, right?" I said softly, leaning closer to Brittney as I turned to face the wall of bottles.

"Yes, but I have faith. I don't believe they could stand a chance against you." She ran her hand across my bicep, squeezing encouragingly before stepping away. I pick one up and stepped back a couple of feet. Zeroing in on the target, I wound up and threw as hard as I could. The ball hit the bottle with a resounding smack, and the glass shattered.

Brittney jumped up and down clapping. "One gone."

I glanced at her with a grin. She seemed very confident I could pull this off. I picked up another ball and threw again with the same result. She repeated her happy dance. I loved watching her.

"Last one," I said, giving her a suggestive look. "I think maybe I need a kiss for good luck."

"You don't need luck," she replied, practically skipping over to place a quick peck against my lips. "You're Chase Walker, one of the best throwing arms around. You have *so* got this!"

"Great." I laughed, giving her a quick smack on the behind. "So now you're betting my career on this as well, are you?"

"Nope. I know you'll succeed." She grinned as she walked away.

I shook my head and turned back toward the target. Focusing for a moment, I threw the ball hard, smashing the third bottle.

"Winner!" the man in the booth shouted and grabbed a hook he had leaning against the wall while Britt squealed in delight. "Which one would you like?"

I deferred to her.

"The white one of course," she said. "White is one of my favorite colors."

I grinned. "Is it now? Since when?"

"Since always. Haven't you noticed all the white furniture in my house? Or have I been keeping you too . . . preoccupied for things like that?"

This was true, I realized as I pondered in surprise. I'd never really paid attention before, but she did have a lot of white things. We had something else is common.

"Here you go, miss." The Carnie handed her the

giant pillow pet, which I thought was supposed to be a cat, perhaps, and she danced around with glee.

"Thank you, Chase! Thank you, thank you, thank you!" She had to crane her head around the dang huge thing to be able to kiss me, and I laughed again. It was almost bigger than she was.

"We're gonna have to go home now, so we don't have to haul this thing around the rest of the night. What would we have done with it on all those rides you dragged me on? I guess it's a good thing we decided to play the games last, huh?"

"Probably. I knew you would win. Come on, let's go find which game Brett and Tana are at and see how they're doing."

I took the massive stuffed beast from her, trying to find a comfortable way to carry it, but it wasn't possible. I finally settled on hooking my arms around its middle, and Brittney slipped her hand in at my elbow, so we could still stroll together.

"You're gonna have to share with me, you know that, right? I worked hard for this . . . ," I studied it again for a second, "cat—dog—creature thing."

"Of course I'll share. What fun is a giant pillow if you have no one to cuddle with? And it's definitely a cat. I'm positive."

"Well, I'm glad one of us is," I replied with a grin.

We saw Brett and Tana standing at a booth the next row over, tossing wiffle balls at a table of brightly colored squares. "You won!" Tana said, pointing excitedly to the yellow winner square the ball was in.

"Here you go. You can choose from any prize in this bucket," the gamer lady said. Tana reached in and pulled a small, brightly-colored, stuffed fish about the size of her hand from the container. "Thank you!" She kissed Brett on the cheek, and the two of them turned around to find us watching.

Brett hung his head in defeat before looking up at me again. "I'd ask you how you did, but the answer is plainly obvious. I swear no matter what I do, you always manage to show me up."

I grinned. "At the moment I'd be quite happy to trade with you. I'd much rather carry the fish around for the rest of the night."

Tana laughed. "No deal! We worked hard for this fish, and I love it. It's the most expensive stuffed animal I've ever owned."

We laughed and turned toward the midway.

"Shall we get something to eat now?" Britt asked. "I swear these smells are about to kill me."

"Food sounds good to me too," Tana added. "I'm starving."

We ended up stopping at a fry bread stand. Brett and I ordered Indian Tacos, and the girls got Strawberry Shortcake fry bread. Brittney carried my plate as we walked toward the picnic tables set up around the outer edge of the grandstand, where a local rock band called Cages was playing some pretty decent music. I deposited the pillow monstrosity on the far end of the table and slid in next to Brittney.

"So did you have a good time tonight?" I asked before taking a bite. I already knew the answer, but I loved hearing her rant on and on about it.

"Oh my gosh, Chase! I'm glad you brought me. I had no idea what I've been missing! It was amazing—you were amazing!" She wrapped her arms around my shoulders and hugged me.

"I'm getting the impression you think it was amazing—not sure, though." I kissed the side of her face. "I'm happy you enjoyed it."

She released me to take a bite of food. "Holy cow! This is divine!"

"I know, right?" Tana replied, licking her lips as she

made a delighted expression. "I'm thinking we need to try to recreate this at home."

"Definitely. I never would've thought to do this. You have to try it, Chase." She cut a bite off and lifted it to my mouth. I took it, and the sweet flavor exploded against my taste buds.

"Mmm. Wow," I said when I finished chewing. "That really is awesome. I think we should tell my grandma about this."

"Oh, your grandma! I bet she'd find a way to improve it," Brett said with a dreamy look. "You have no idea how much I miss her."

"I have every idea. She'd be appalled by the things we've been eating lately."

"This is true."

"You should let us cook for you all the time," Tana said. "Britt and I may not rival your grandma, but I'd wager we cook way better than the two of you."

"I wouldn't ever say no to you girls' cooking," I said quickly. I was sick of pizza. "I've loved the few meals you've made for us in the past. Heck, if you wanted to make a week's worth of meals, I'd pay for the ingredients. I think it's only fair for Brett and I to pay if you're doing all the work."

"I think it would be fun to start having meals together all the time. I mean, we do go out a lot together, but this would feel so . . . family like. Even if it's only dinner every night, that would be fine with me," Britt added.

"Let's do it," I agreed, and we spent the next several minutes coming up with dinner ideas the girls could buy groceries for.

"We better get hustling," Brett said after a while, glancing at his phone. "Chase and I have weights again in the morning."

"Correction—you have weights in the morning. I'm

not allowed to go until I receive a call from coach with clearance," I reminded. "But you're right. Everyone has an early start. We should call it a night."

I stood, stacking Brittney's and my empty plates together and heading toward the garbage can while everyone else gathered their things.

"Well, look who it is, Mr. Dope Addict," a familiar voice said, and I turned around to find Matt and Jared standing there with a couple of girls I didn't know. They glanced between the three of us uneasily.

"Don't start with me, Matt. You, out of everyone, know exactly how bogus those charges are." I was going to try to remain calm.

"And what if I do? You can't prove anything." He folded his arms and glared.

"Really? Did you remember to wear gloves when you tampered with my locker?" I asked, calling his bluff, and he fidgeted nervously, a telltale sign which let me know for sure he was the guilty party. "How about when you bashed up my truck?"

His eyes darted in Jared's direction before looking at me.

"He don't got nothin' on us," Jared said, shouldering forward. "If he did, the cops would be swarming all over us by now."

"Dude, you really are friggin' stupid," Brett said, coming up beside me followed closely by Tana and Brittney. "You practically admitted you're responsible. If you're gonna commit a crime, you might wanna learn to lie better. Come on, Chase. Let the police deal with them. They aren't worth your time."

I started to walk away, but Brittney stepped forward. "Is it true? Did you do those awful things?"

"What I do or don't do is none of your business anymore, now is it? Run along with your new boy toy, and when you're ready for a real man again, you know where to find me. At least there's no chance of you dying in a car accident if you sneak out to meet him, since he lives next door. How convenient."

The comment struck me like a ton of bricks, and in the blink of an eye I was ready to take his head off, but Brittney put her hand on my chest, stopping me.

"He's more man than you'll ever be," she spat. "I hope I never lay eyes on you again, Matt. Chase has been through hell because of Nikki. Don't you have any respect for the dead? I had no idea you were so sick and twisted."

He laughed and stared at me. "I bet it burns you to know I had her first, doesn't it?"

I stepped forward, and Brett grabbed my arm in warning, but I shrugged him off, knowing there were two DPS officers on fair patrol who were starting to watch our discussion with interest. "If that's true, then it doesn't say much for you, does it? If you were any good, she'd still be with you."

My head snapped back as he punched me hard, and I laughed, grabbing his fist as he came toward me again. The two DPS officers, who'd been eyeing us, came running forward, commanding us to stop. The girls with Matt and Jared held up their hands as they backed away. Jared looked at me furiously.

One of the officers grabbed Matt, pulling his arms behind and cuffing him.

"Do you want to press assault charges?" the cop asked me.

"I most certainly do. These two have been involved in other harassment cases against me."

"They weren't my ideas," Jared said, as the second officer approached him. "They were his!" He pointed to Matt, and I couldn't help but grin again. They were cooking their own goose.

One of the policemen briefly spoke into his radio,

calling for backup before addressing me again. "We're going to need all of you to come to the security office to give statements."

"That's fine with me," I replied. "And could you please call my football coach? He needs to hear this too."

"Your football coach?" He squinted his eyes as he studied my face. "Oh my gosh! You're Chase Walker, aren't you?"

"That would be me."

"I'm a huge fan. Man, it sucked you weren't at the game yesterday. You feeling better?" His whole demeanor changed from wary to warm and friendly.

"Much better," I said honestly, resisting the urge to laugh when Matt grimaced.

"Well, come on then. Let's go sort this out and get your eye checked by the medics too. It looks like it's gonna be a shiner."

"Okay. Let me grab my things."

"I've got it, Chase," Brett said, shouldering his sister's giant pillow pet. "Lead the way."

~Chapter Twenty-Three~

"You want me to do what?" I asked, giving her a skeptical look.

"Play paint twister. Come on, it'll be fun! This is a huge competition one of the sorority houses is putting on. They'll love being able to boast that the star quarterback is at their party."

"Explain the rules. How exactly do you play?" I looked across the wide expanse of lawn at the many Twister games spread across the ground.

"It's easy. It's like regular twister, but they put the same color paint in each circle, so wherever you touch, that color of paint gets on you."

"It sounds, messy—and slippery—and wet."

"Precisely, all while you're tangled up with a bunch of girls. This is why I told you to wear old clothes you didn't mind getting ruined."

Okay, the idea did have some fun merit, but I still felt iffy. "I don't want to be tangled up with a bunch of girls, just you."

"I'll be there too, but the only way you can stay with me, is if the two of us keep on beating everyone else. There will be two couples on each sheet. One of us has to be the last one standing to win the game, then we advance to the next round. They spray off the sheets in between each match and repaint them again."

"So what's the prize for winning?"

"A new car! Look, it's over there. They got one of the big dealerships down here to donate, because the sorority president is his niece or something."

I glanced in the direction she was pointing, and spotted the cute, maroon compact car with a small Sun Devil logo and thin yellow stripes painted on the side. "Love the paint job." I grinned. "It's sick."

"Wouldn't I look great driving up to watch you play games in it? It's like the perfect accessory for your girlfriend. I could *so* use a new car, Chase. I have to borrow or ask for rides from Brett, Tana, or you."

"This is going to be a disaster," I replied, shaking my head.

"So you'll do it?"

"Of course I will. You need a car." Didn't she know she had me wrapped around her finger? I'd give in and do anything for her.

"Yay!" she squealed and threw her arms around my neck jumping up and down. "I love you so much! You're the best boyfriend ever."

I laughed and kissed her lightly on the mouth. "You might want to wait to thank me. We haven't actually won yet."

"We will! I have faith!"

I laughed. "Glad someone does. Where do we need to sign up?"

She bit her lip and blushed. "I already did."

"What? Without asking me? What if I had said no?"

"I'm fairly confident in my persuasion skills when it comes to you."

"Hmm. Sounds like I should've put up a harder fight."

"Too late now," she replied in a singsong voice. "Come here and sit down. Let's take our shoes off."

I followed her to a stone bench and sat beside her. "I hope I don't catch my death of cold from doing this. The breeze tonight is a bit on the chilly side."

"I heard it was supposed to snow in the mountains tomorrow." she replied. "I talked to my mom earlier today. She said it's been really cold and windy up there."

"I definitely don't miss that."

"You don't like the snow?"

"I don't mind it so much, I just don't care for the storm blowing in. I swear that howling wind nearly drove me mad at times."

"Yeah, I don't miss the wind either."

I looked at the massive amount of students gathered on the lawn. "How many couples entered this thing?"

"A bunch! I'm not sure how many."

"Sounds like a lot of games of Twister to me."

"As long as we keep winning, yes. I'm thinking the paint will make things go quicker, though, because it's harder to stay up."

"True. By the way, how the heck will we get home? We'll have paint all over us. I don't want it to get on everything."

"I brought us extra clothes, and they've opened the showers at the pool, so people can clean up. That's why they're doing it right here."

"You've had this planned for a while now, haven't you?"

She nodded guiltily. "I have. I didn't tell you what was happening, because I was afraid you'd say no. But if I said it was a date—I knew you'd never pass that up."

"Well, aren't you the sneaky little devil?" I grinned and gave her a wink.

"Sneaky little Sun Devil to you, and I'm gonna be driving that Sun Devil car too!" She jumped up, grabbing my hand. "Let's go. People are starting to get in line."

She dragged me to where a tall girl with glasses was staring at a list of names, checking them off as people came forward, and directing them where to go.

"Brittney Dodson and Chase Walker," Britt told her.

She found us on the list. "You're at game sheet number ten against Rocky Dane and Robyn Sheraton. Go stand on the end opposite them, and wait for further instructions."

"Oh, I'm incredibly excited," Britt said, bouncing along as if she'd eaten a five pound bag of sugar.

"Why?" I asked unable to help my chuckle at how hyper she was.

"Because it's gonna be so much fun, and I have the best athlete on campus as my partner. There's no way we can lose!"

"I should probably remind you—rolling in paint isn't exactly my athletic specialty."

"Maybe not, but you're strong, muscular, and probably in better shape than most the people here. That's gotta count for something."

"We'll find out soon, I guess, won't we?"

"Yes, we will." She rubbed her hands together with glee.

A sharp whistle blew, and a stylishly dressed brunette climbed on a footstool with a mike in her hand. "Hi, all! My name is Irene Winsor, and I want to welcome everyone to our event this evening! It's a tad cool tonight, I know, but we still plan on having lots of fun. First off, here are the rules. To make it fair, everyone will be playing the exact same game, which will be called over this microphone. Please pay attention, because we won't be repeating. When a color and limb are called, you will move your corresponding body part to that color circle. The object of the game is to keep your butt, knees, and elbows from touching the ground as you move to the new spot without pulling any of your other limbs off the spot they're currently on. If you do, you're disqualified and must leave the game. If your partner loses too, then you're out of the competition. If you or your partner wins the game, then you go on to the next round. There will be two judges watching each game to see who falls and is out.

"As you know, we have a tricked out Sun Devil car to give away tonight, sponsored by Hot Vehicles of Tempe. Let's give them a round of applause for their generous donation."

Everyone clapped, and there were a few whistles and cheers as well.

"Okay, let's win a car!"

Another girl stepped beside Irene and spun the board showing her the result. "Left foot, blue!" Irene called, and we stepped onto the mat.

"Hey, how ya doin?" I asked politely, shaking the hands of the other two we were facing, and exchanged pleasant hellos.

"Nothing like getting up close and personal on the first date is there?" Rocky joked, and we laughed.

"No kidding," I replied. "But I'm used to a team of strangers wanting to tackle me, so I'm okay with this, I guess. It's gotta be a lot less painful."

"I'd imagine that would be true."

"Right foot, yellow," came the next command, and we easily complied, though I had to say I wasn't really loving the feel of paint squishing between my toes.

Britt wrinkled her nose. "It's slimier than I thought it would feel. Kinda icky."

"Remember, this is all your fault, sweetheart." I grinned.

"Right hand, yellow."

Now things were going to start getting tricky. We scrambled for the closest available spot. Robyn was the unlucky person who had to reach the farthest from where she was. She slipped and fell.

"Out!" one of our judges called, and I heard the same echo from a few other mats as well.

"Hang in there, Rocky!" Robyn encouraged as she stood and left the plastic, wiping her hands on her pants as she went.

"Left hand, red!"

I had to contort my body to reach this one, and I could feel myself sliding in the paint, damn stuff. I'd be fine if it wasn't involved. I gritted my teeth, torn between laughing and growling as I tried to stay up.

"If you fall, it'll be me knotted up with him for the rest of the game," Brittney whispered in my ear.

"Are you trying to give me extra incentive? Because while that might normally work, I can't see how it's going to keep me from slipping through paint."

She had the audacity to giggle at my comment. "Aren't you having fun?"

"Loads," I replied as I fell to the ground.

"Out," a judge called, and I got up, pausing first to smack Britt firmly on the butt, so she'd have my handprint there for the rest of the night.

"Ouch!" she said in surprise. "What was that for?"

"Marking my territory," I said with a laugh. "Pay attention or you're going to lose on the first round."

Her face was a mask of determination as I watched her play the rest of the game, and in the end, it paid off. She won, and we were moving on.

Things were quickly reset, and the games continued. Set by set, several couples were eliminated, but somehow, Britt and I managed to keep going. We ran fairly even, both of us being the last one standing many times, and on several occasions, we were left there together. In those cases we didn't have to finish the match because we'd already won. It was nice to take a break. It might be a silly game, but it was proving to be a strenuous workout all the same. It had been quite a feat to hold myself in some of the jumbled positions I'd ended up in. If I were being truthful, this crazy event had kicked my competitive nature into overdrive. Car or not, I was determined to win this thing—just to prove I could.

Finally, we managed to make it all the way to the last match. Britt and I looked like we'd been cast in a zombie movie or something—we were so splotched and covered in paint. It was everywhere; in my hair, all over my bare skin, and I was fairly certain some of it had managed to creep into my underwear somehow. I couldn't wait to hit the shower. I hoped this stuff would come off easily.

The two people we were facing didn't look nearly as bad as we did. This made me nervous because it could only mean they hadn't fallen as much as we had. Both the guy and the girl were in pretty good shape. Our work was cut out for us.

"Chase," Britt said, catching my attention.

"Yeah?"

"Kiss me for good luck."

I grinned and wrapped my painted limbs around her, pulling her close and giving her a resounding, full kiss—one which started the onlookers cheering and catcalling. She wrapped her arms around me and kissed me vigorously, and I couldn't help my widening smile as the crowd started chanting, "Walker, Walker, Walker," over and over again.

"I think you're the crowd favorite to win," Brittney said as she pulled away, laughing.

"*We* are the crowd favorite to win. Come on, let's finish this and take your car home. I'm tired."

"Deal."

We stepped onto the mat and shook the hands of our opponents, named Ryan and Megan.

"So, I'm guessing this is your girlfriend," Ryan said as he turned to Brittney.

"Nah, she's my sister," I replied, deadpan.

Ryan's head snapped in my direction, his eyes wide.

"Gotcha," I said, snapping my fingers, hoping maybe I'd thrown him off his mental game a bit.

He laughed. "You did there for a second. I guess it was kind of a dumb question. Megan is my girlfriend as well, and we are both big fans of yours. It's a pleasure to umm . . . twist with you tonight."

"Thanks, man—I think." I shook my head, chuckling at how perverse that sounded.

The whistle blew, and the game began.

"Right hand, green." Great, we were going to have to bend over already.

"Left foot, blue." Stretched clear across the mat.

"Left hand, yellow." Getting increasingly difficult as we scrambled for placement.

"Right foot, red."

Megan went down, and I felt a moment of elation when the judge called her out. Two of us against one—this game was ours. My confidence was shattered in the next moment as I heard Britt yelp behind me.

"No!" she exclaimed.

"Out!" the judge called.

Shoot! It was down to us guys. I had to win this car for Brittney. It would kill her if we got this close only to lose now.

"Right hand, red," the next position was called, and Ryan and I continued to battle for several turns until we were both in a precariously balanced position. My limbs were shaking with effort as I tried to hold my spot. I could also feel his trembling where we had contact.

His hand slipped a little, causing more of his weight to fall onto me since he was angled across my back. My grip slid and I fell, unable to hold it any longer, and Ryan collapsed on top of me. A collective gasp rang through the crowd. I'd lost.

"Good game, man," Ryan said, holding out his hand

and helping me to my feet. "I'm sorry about that. My slipping caused you to fall, I think."

"No worries. I hit the ground first. Rules are rules."

"We have a winner folks," Irene's voice came through the loud speaker.

"I'm so sorry," I said as I approached Brittney. "I really tried."

"It wasn't your fault," she said, wrapping her arms around me and kissing my now paint covered lips.

"Can I have Ryan and Megan, and Chase and Brittney come here please?" Irene asked.

I grabbed Brittney's hand, and the four of us walked over together.

"We'd like to thank everyone for participating tonight. It's been a fun event! What did you think of the last match?"

There was a burst of cheers and applause from the crowd.

"What many of you failed to notice, was Ryan and Megan didn't participate in all the matches. That's because they're ringers from the car dealership we slipped in to make things a bit more fun. So, that means, Chase and Brittney, you're the winners of the new car!"

"What?" Brittney exclaimed before throwing her arms around me and jumping up and down. "Oh my gosh! We did it, we did it, we did it!"

"I'd say that deserves another kiss. Don't you think so?"

The crowd roared its approval, and even if they hadn't, nothing was gonna stop me from kissing my girl.

~Chapter Twenty-Four~

"I have half a mind to make you personally scrub off every bit of paint left on me when we get home. I've been in the dang shower for almost forty-five minutes trying to remove all this stuff. There's still some in my hair. Thank goodness they used water based paint."

Brittney laughed and reached up to ruffle her fingers along the top of my head. "I think the paint flecks look good. It's like rainbow colored dandruff."

"You aren't helping things. I don't want dandruff of any color, and your hair looks as bad as mine does."

She giggled and wrapped her arms around my neck, popping up on her tiptoes to kiss me lightly. "Relax. Someone told me you can rub olive oil through your hair, and it will strip the paint off."

"Well, then I say we stop by a store on the way home and pick some up."

"I'll be driving my new car home, remember?" She dangled the keys happily in front of me.

"That's right. Are you going to follow me to the store?"

"Would you mind getting it? Tana is dying to see the car. I told her I'd hurry."

"It'd probably be for the best anyway. You shouldn't be driving it all over the place until you get your insurance set up. I can help you do that tomorrow."

"Thank you again, Chase. You know, technically this car belongs to you as much as it does to me. I couldn't have done it without you."

I pulled her against me. "Nah, I want you to have it.

I have my truck, and besides, you deserve it." I brushed my thumb over some yellow paint specks on her face, which gave her the appearance of having light freckles. "I love you."

"I love you too." She rose and pressed her lips to mine. I didn't think I'd ever get enough kisses from her. Every second I spent with her tied her further to my heart. I slid a hand into her hair, holding her mouth to mine as our tongues met, leaning together as we feathered light strokes over one another.

We broke apart and I grinned. "You better get going. I've been twisted up with you on this grass all night. I have no problem doing it again."

She smiled. "I thought you were cold."

"You took care of that."

"Hmm." She bit her lip and cast a suggestive look over me.

"Leave," I ordered, pointing to her new vehicle.

She sighed and started walking away. "Okay, but maybe we can pick up where we left off when you get home?"

"Most definitely."

"See you in a few."

"Hey. I'll be a little while, okay? I've got to gas up my truck before I go to the store and run by Coach's office. He asked me to come sign some papers tonight. He said he'd be in until eleven o'clock."

"Don't keep me waiting too long."

"I'll be there as fast as I can." I watched as she started her car, and when she drove past, she gave an excited wave, pure joy written on her face.

"Hi, Coach. Sorry I'm late getting here. I got sidetracked tonight."

He glanced at me. "Painting something?"

I chuckled. "Not exactly. I've been helping my

girlfriend win a car."

"Ah! The sorority event they held tonight. I remember hearing something about it. So you won?"

"We did, thank goodness. It'll make wearing this paint around for the next week worth it."

He laughed. "I'm sure it'll help. Have a seat."

I did as he asked, wondering what was going on.

"As you know, both Matt and Jared confessed to being involved with setting you up. There was a hearing between the school board and their lawyer, and there's been a plea bargain of sorts. The school agreed to expel them in lieu of pressing formal charges of tampering and harassment. They still have to go through a regular hearing to see what their legal punishment will be, but as far as the school is concerned, this ends our involvement in the case. In regards to you, the school would like you to sign a document stating you know nothing of, nor have you participated in the use or sale of illegal substance while a part of this institution. If you'll agree, then the school's investigative proceedings will be closed, and we can wash our hands and move on."

"Where do I sign?" I answered immediately. I was anxious to get this over with.

Coach relaxed visibly. "I have the statement here." He slid a manila folder across his desk, handing me a pen also.

I leaned forward and read through the document before I signed and slid it toward him. He checked it while I glanced around the room at the numerous triangular football banners which hung about the windows of the room. There were several trophies from various season and events displayed in a case behind his desk. I wondered if we'd ever get anything like that this year.

"This is good," he replied, sliding the folder into his

desk. "I appreciate your willingness to cooperate. I didn't want you to feel like you were getting shortchanged."

"I don't feel that way at all. I'm happy to be done with it."

"Hopefully the two of them have learned their lesson and won't bother you anymore."

"I agree. That would be nice."

"So are you feeling pretty comfortable with everyone else on the team? As odd as this may sound to a guy your age—we don't tolerate bullying here. I want to make sure you aren't feeling threatened in any way.

"No one's bothering me."

"You sure? I noticed Brubaker seems to rub you pretty hard."

"Nothing but healthy rivalry, Coach. He's just upset I got picked as the starter instead of him. Don't talk to him about it. The competition helps keep me on my toes."

"You deserve the spot, Chase. Don't let anyone tell you otherwise. We have lots of good players on the team, but regardless of class and age, the best man will always get first pick for the job. You showed great strength and determination during the practice season. Frankly, I've been thrilled to see you get this shot. I think you could really go places."

"Thanks. I enjoy playing. I promise to keep working hard, and I'm sorry for the drama that's revolved around me."

"Not your fault. I'm sorry I had to sideline you until we discovered the results for sure."

"I understand. No hard feelings."

"Good. Now get outta here, so I can go home. I'll see you at practice tomorrow."

"Will do. Have a good night."

I left the locker room feeling lighter than I had in a

long time. I got in my truck and headed to the store for the oil Brittney suggested, grabbing a few other items I needed before checking out.

Not wanting Brittney to worry about me, I decided to text her and explain why I was running so late. However, when I reached for my phone, I discovered it wasn't in my pocket.

"Great," I muttered, patting my other pockets as I walked toward the parking lot. I must've left it in the truck. I popped the lock and looked in the cup holder, but it wasn't there either, so I checked between and under the seats. "Where the hell did it go?"

I mentally retraced my steps—trying to remember the last time I'd used it. It had been right before the Twister game when Coach had called, asking me to come by. I'd set it inside one of my shoes when I'd taken them off. I didn't remember picking it up again. I must've fallen out there.

Grumbling, I headed back toward the school. The place was completely deserted now, no evidence we'd been here earlier, other than some smashed grass. I parked and walked to where we'd sat. Here and there I noticed splotches of paint which hadn't been washed away, and I grinned to myself. What a crazy night.

Pausing at the stone bench, I bent to check underneath. Sure enough, there was my phone. I sighed in relief, grateful to have found it, and picked it up. The alert light was blinking, and I clicked it to see what I'd missed.

There were several calls, actually, from Brett. I clicked open the dialer to call when my phone started buzzing again. It was him.

"Hey, man," I answered.

"Where have you been? Why haven't you answered your phone?" He sounded both relieved and agitated.

"Sorry, bro. I lost it and had to retrace my steps to

find it. I swear I barely picked it up when you called. What's up?"

Brett sighed heavily. "I have something to tell you, but I don't want you to freak out, okay?"

"That's not going to help keep me calm." I felt my nerves ratchet up a notch. "What's wrong?"

"Brittney was in a car accident on her way home."

The world dipped and swooned in front of me as memories from the night of Nikki's accident crashed over me like tidal waves. I sat down on the bench with a thud. "How bad?" I felt sick—ready to vomit. Beads of sweat broke out on my forehead, and I started trembling.

"I'm not sure yet. The officer on the phone said he couldn't give me any information other than she was injured and had been taken by ambulance to the hospital. He said the accident happened about an hour ago."

Right after she'd left me. "Where'd they take her?"

"Tempe St. Luke's."

"I'll be there in five minutes. Don't you leave her alone, Brett. Do you hear me? Don't you leave her alone!"

"I'm already here—on my way into the emergency room right now."

"Tell her I'm coming." I ended the call, standing to head blindly toward my truck before switching directions and running toward one of the stationary garbage bins near the sidewalk.

I puked.

~Chapter Twenty-Five~

I checked in with the lady at the emergency room desk. "I'm here to see my girlfriend who was brought in by ambulance." I couldn't make my voice stop shaking. "She was in a car accident."

She directed me to the rows of empty chairs and said she'd let someone know. Brett must've already gone back, and there was no way in hell I was going to sit here doing nothing, so I went into the bathroom nearby to rinse my mouth and splash some water on my face.

"Get a grip, Walker," I said to my reflection as I dripped over the sink. There was a knot in my throat I couldn't swallow, and tears were close to the surface. It was all I could do to hold it together.

I dried my face and returned to the waiting room. I tried dialing Brett's number, but it went straight to message. I walked toward the desk to ask again, but the receptionist stood before I got there, stepping around the corner out of sight. I waited for her to return.

"Marge," I heard her speak to an unseen individual. "I have a young man here who wants to see his girlfriend. She was brought in by ambulance from the car accident."

"Is she the one who died? I'll need to get the doctor," a new voice answered. My mouth went dry, and my tongue suddenly seemed swollen. I thought I was going to vomit again.

No, no, no, NO! My blood roared in my ears, drowning all other sound, and I ran outside, barely clearing the doorway before I was overtaken with great gulping sobs. My heart was being ripped from my chest . . . again.

I felt like someone was punching me repeatedly in the gut as I hurried to my truck, desperate to escape, but instead, I halted when I reached it, bracing myself. In my mind I saw Nikki, Brittney, Nikki, the images flashing back and forth as if they were being clicked with a repeat button.

"I . . . I . . . I can't do this again! I won't survive this time!" I was going to explode. My heart pounded in my ears, and I didn't know what to do—I only knew I was going to lose it.

When had I let it happen? When had I broken my own rule to never let someone get this close? There was a reason I'd erected all these defenses—a reason I'd wanted to keep people at arm's length, but no—love had snuck in again with Brittney. She'd already been there, so I let my guard down. I'd set myself up to fall—to be traumatized the same way I had before. I couldn't do it—couldn't. I'd rather die.

I dropped to my knees, slumping over as I grabbed my hair in my fists. "Why?" I screamed into the night air, not caring who might hear me. "Why does this keep happening? What the hell have I done to deserve this?" I wrapped my arms around my waist rocking back and forth. "I can't take anymore!" I shouted. "Do you hear me? God! Whoever you are—whoever is controlling this damn sinking ship—stop doing this!"

I was livid—so incredibly furious! I slammed my fist repeatedly against the pavement; wanting to beat the shit out of something—anything—beat it until *I* was dead. "Why? Why? Why? Somebody answer me, dammit!"

My chin trembled as I shuddered. I wanted the hurt inside to stop. I'd deluded myself into believing I was healed—I had successful moved on—but it wasn't true. I was still a mess, a puddle of weeping misery with no hope for the future. I couldn't go on like this. It was killing me—eating me from the inside out.

I growled as I smashed my hand into the ground one more time splitting my knuckles open. "I'm done, Nikki," I spoke angrily. "I've done everything I promised you I would . . . did everything you thought I should do. You told me life would get better, not worse. You *lied* to me—in the worst way possible—a lie that's taking me apart piece by piece. I'm not any better. I'm going insane because of all this, and now I'm dying the worst kind of death—the death of my soul. I fell in love with her, Nikki! I fell in love with her. She means everything to me—do you hear me—*everything*, and now she's just like you. I friggin' *kill* everything I touch! It would be better if no one had ever met me! Why is this happening again?"

I knelt there, tears dripping to the pavement, hiccupping from crying, waiting, wishing, hoping to hear an answer, but the only sounds were of my heavy breathing and traffic rushing by on the street. All I could see was my eyelashes clumped from tears and the blurred ground in front of me. I couldn't even move to get up. I was exhausted . . . spent.

"Chase?" I heard Brett's voice behind me, but I was afraid to turn and look at him. "Are you okay? The hospital staff said you were in the waiting room, but I didn't see you." I felt his hand on my shoulder. "Talk to me, man."

I didn't look up. "I can't do this again, Brett. I'm sorry, I can't."

He crouched beside me. "Dude, I know you've been to hell and back with stuff like this—that's why I was afraid to call you. Honestly, man, it's nothing to be upset over. They said she might need ten stitches is all."

I yanked my head up, my heart racing a million miles a minute. I didn't dare to hope. "She's okay?"

"Yeah. It was a fairly minor accident—not her fault. She t-boned a car that didn't stop at a sign. Her airbag deployed, and she split the top of her head open against the visor somehow. It bled a lot, but once they cleaned it up, it wasn't as bad as it looked. They said her x-ray was good too.

I grabbed him by the shoulders. "Take me to her *now*." I heard what he was saying, but I was afraid to believe until I saw her with my own eyes. I followed as we hurried into the waiting room. The receptionist was at the desk once again, and she waved us through, clicking a button, which opened the doors into the emergency area. "Where is she?" I asked.

"She's in trauma four," Brett replied.

I ran, without knowing where I was going in the massive place. I started following the numbers overhead.

"Turn left," Brett instructed, keeping pace with me.

There it was, number four. I hurried through the glass doors, brushed the privacy curtain aside, and saw Brittney—*my Brittney*—reclined on the exam bed with a gash on her forehead and blood splatters in her hair.

"Chase." She smiled softly, reaching for me.

I ran to her, grabbing her face in my hands, and I kissed her—hard. "You're all right," I managed to choke out and kissed her again. "Am I hurting you?" I kissed her again, and she started laughing when I stepped back to run my hands over her, checking her.

"I'm okay, really."

"Your arms and neck are bruised," I stated, pausing to kiss them too.

"Airbag," she replied simply. "Talk to me, Chase. You've been crying, I can tell. I'm so sorry. I know this probably did a real number on you."

"I'm okay . . . *now*. I overhead some of the staff talking about a girl who'd been in a car accident, and they said she'd died. I thought I had lost you too. I wanted to die myself." I took her face and kissed her again, deeply this time, a bit frantic at first but then slower and more languid.

"Breathe," she instructed me when I pulled away. "Everything is going to be fine." She stroked the side of my face, and I leaned into her embrace, incredibly grateful for her touch.

I placed my hand over hers, holding it there against me, briefly closing my eyes to marvel in the feel of her. A tear escaped, running down my cheek, and she brushed it away. "I don't ever want to lose you."

"You won't. I'll be here as long as you want me." Her thumb continued to move against my cheek.

"I'll always want you—always." An idea struck me, and I ran with it. "Let's get married, Britt." I heard Brett make a choking sound behind me.

Her eyes widened, and she laughed in surprise. "Are you serious? You know you aren't supposed to make life-altering decisions when you're under stress. I think this qualifies as one of those times."

"That may be true," I replied stepping closer, so I could take her face in my hands again. "But I already know how much I love you, and I don't ever want to be apart again . . . ever. Let's do it."

"You are serious! We're only nineteen," she squeaked glancing over at Brett before looking back. "What will our families say? We've barely started college! And there's your football career."

"None of it means anything without you. I've learned life is too short to keep hoping for someday to arrive. If you need time, then we'll take time—get married in a year, after we both turn twenty. Whatever, I don't care. I just want to know you're mine."

"I *am* yours already. There's never been any doubt about that for me."

I bent and kissed her lips. "Then say yes. I've never wanted anything in my life as much as I want you." I knew the words were the truth when I spoke them. It amazed me how much things had changed in the last few months.

Her eyes misted as she stared at me, searching. "Do you really mean that?"

"Every single bit. I love you, Brittney, more than anything."

She kissed me this time, and I loved the feel of her against my mouth. She pulled away, nodding as tears slowly fell. "Then yes, I'll marry you."

I couldn't help the smile spreading over my face. "You're amazing. Please remember this answer when I ask you for real—with all the candlelight and romance. I don't want you to tell our kids about my lame proposal in an emergency room." I leaned in to kiss her again, but she placed her fingers over my lips, stopping me.

"Don't you dare propose to me again, Chase Walker. This is the most romantic scenario than any girl could ever dream. It's perfect." She grinned. "I *want* to tell our kids about this."

We were talking about kids—our kids. Incredible. "Well, then at least let me give you a fancy celebration dinner." I brushed my thumb across her beautiful lips, noting the bits of bruising on her face too. Even injured she was still the most beautiful girl I'd ever seen.

"I can do that, I guess." We kissed again, but were interrupted when the nurse came in to check on her. I stepped away so she could take her vitals and turned to glance at Brett who was beaming.

He clapped me in a bear hug. "Welcome to the family, bro."

"It's gonna be brothers for real now," I replied with

a grin.

"I gotta say—I'm thrilled. It may have happened sooner than I expected, but I'm really happy for you both. You're good together."

"I love her, man. I promise I'll take good care of her," I said stepping away.

"I know you will, or I'll kick your butt." We both laughed.

"Hey, do you have some tape and a pen I could borrow real quick?" I asked the nurse. She gave me a funny look but handed me some from her pocket. I wrote on the tape and broke a piece off, going around to the other side of the bed. I took Brittney's hand and wrapped it around her ring finger.

She laughed and lifted it so she could see it.

"It says, reserved for Chase." I grabbed her hand and kissed it. She laughed, clasping her other hand to her heart as she studied it.

The nurse lifted her eyebrows in question. "Did I miss something?"

"Yep," Brittney said with a grin. "We just got engaged."

~Epilogue~

4 years later-

I brushed her hair away from her damp forehead. "You're beautiful. You know that, right?"

She grimaced, panting. "I don't believe you."

"Well, you should. I don't think I've seen you look prettier than you do right now."

She moaned louder. "Another one is starting. I can feel it."

I grabbed her leg and helped push her knee back like her mom was doing on the other side.

"Here we go!" the doctor said. "Now push! Yes, come on, come on, come on. Keep going, a little longer. Keep going!"

"I can't. I can't! It's too hard! I'm too tired!" she exclaimed.

"Come on, Brittney. You can do this. You're tough. Don't give up now!" I encouraged.

"I can see the head crowning. We're almost there!" the doctor said. "One more big push should do it."

"You can do it, babe. Come on!"

Brittney scrunched her face up and bore down hard, her pretty features turning red from the effort.

"Yes, yes!" the doctor called. "Here it comes!"

The baby's head popped out, and the doctor quickly turned it, allowing the rest of the body to easily slide into his waiting hands.

"It's a girl!" he pronounced confirming what we'd been told during our ultrasound months earlier. "Congratulations! You're both officially parents!"

I couldn't help my proud smile as I bent over to kiss

my wife on the forehead. "She's here! You did it. You were amazing."

She squeezed my hand and started crying. We both turned to stare as the baby uttered a very healthy wail. "She's so pretty," she choked.

"Future cheerleader–like her mom. Would you listen to those lungs?" I grinned happily.

"Is daddy cutting the cord?" the nurse asked.

"Yes, I am," I replied, taking the scissors she handed me. I tried not to shake as I carefully cut between the two clamps.

The nurse wiped the baby off with a towel before picking her up and moving to the warmer while the doctor continued to attend to Brittney. I watched as they weighed and cleaned her up better. She was so tiny, flailing her little fingers and toes while she cried and kicked about.

I had a daughter. She was never going to be allowed to date. So help me if a boy even came near her, I was pulling out my shotgun.

The nurse swaddled her nice and tight in a blanket and handed her to me. "I'll let daddy take this sweet girl to her mommy."

I was terrified–so afraid I'd drop her. She was so small, nuzzling against me trustingly, and I realized I was responsible for her. It was up to me to make sure she was loved and cared for–had the best life I could give her. It was overwhelming. I lifted her up and placed a kiss against her forehead. How was it possible to love someone this instantly?

"You look really good with her," Brittney said softly, an exhausted smile splayed across her face. "Thick as thieves already, I can see."

All of a sudden I was choked up. Moments of my life flashed before my eyes, times of feeling destitute and unworthy to continue–all the times I'd considered ending my life because the pain seemed too unbearable. Look at what I would've missed if I'd followed through, continuing in my downward spiral. I couldn't believe the darkness had turned to such light—my broken heart had healed and now loved to capacity. I couldn't believe how wonderful everything was . . . as if it had all been leading to this very moment when a family—*my* family—had been born from the most intense love.

I felt a brief second of panic, realizing if I'd made the wrong choices, I'd never have gotten to this point. I was overwhelmed with what the love of two beautiful young ladies had done to transform me. I'd never been as happy as I was right now. I'd never felt more complete. Everything I'd gone through had been worth it—made perfect by this moment.

"Do we have a name picked for the baby yet?" the nurse asked, interrupting my flash of revelation.

I looked at Brittney, and she smiled, giving me a nod to go ahead and tell her.

"Yes we do," I replied. Tears welled in my eyes as I stared at my newborn child. "Her name is Nikki Lynn Walker."

~My Story~

I've had several readers ask me about this book, wanting to know what was real in the story, so I thought I'd share a few of those things.

I lost my boyfriend, Mike, to a tragic accident when I was 18 and he was 19 years old. We hadn't known each other as long as Chase and Nikki; in fact we had only known each other for a month or so when it happened.

We met one night through mutual friends and hit it off instantly—visiting for hours, and even holding hands. The connection between us was that fast. He asked me to go out later that evening, but due to a misunderstanding on a meeting location, we failed to hook up. (This was in the prehistoric days before cell phone use, so we couldn't call each other to correct that.) I was pretty bummed because he lived three hours away, and I knew we wouldn't have the opportunity to see one another very often.

He came by the next morning before he left town with his friend and asked if he could please have my phone number, so we could stay in touch. I excitedly said yes, and we visited as long as we could, holding hands until he had to go, and then he hugged me goodbye.

He called me as soon as he got home, (this was also the days of no free long distance,) and we began our over-the-phone relationship. We racked up hundreds and hundreds of dollars worth of calls, talking to each other for hours every single day. I think we covered every topic under the sun—from what kinds of food we liked, to eventual marriage. It was a strange relationship, because we hadn't spent much time together physically, but we knew we were in love and had told each other so.

I greatly enjoyed visiting with him, listening to his opinions and sharing his dreams and insights on life. I think my heart raced every second we were on the phone together, and when it would come time to hang up, neither of us wanted to be the one to end the call. We would laugh as each of us waited for the other to go first, but it never happened. When the calls actually ended, I'd lay on the floor with my hand over my chest and a stupid, silly grin on my face as I thought about everything we'd talked about.

My roommate and I shared cars with her parents, but we didn't have our own car, so it wasn't convenient to take off and go somewhere. However, I was finally able to arrange a time to see him. A cousin of mine was getting married about an hour away from where Mike lived, and we made arrangements to meet and spend the weekend together. He wanted me to meet his family and get to know them while I was there, and I knew it would be a big turning point in our relationship. I was really excited.

I talked to him the night before we left and told him I'd call him the next day when we reached our hotel. My best friend and I had a blast together on the way, singing and being silly, looking forward to hooking up with everyone. When we reached the hotel, I called Mike's house. His sister answered the phone, and I asked for him. I'll never forget her words:

"I'm sorry. Michael died."

I hung up the phone and stared at it.

My best friend immediately asked me what was wrong. I looked up at her and said I must've got the wrong number, because they told me Mike was dead. I started shaking.

She grabbed the phone and called the number, asking to speak with Mike. She started yelling at the person saying this was not a funny joke, that it was really hurtful, and to put Mike on the phone. That's when they asked if they were speaking to Lacey. My friend identified herself and said I was with her. They apologized and informed her they'd tried to reach us before we left home. They told her Mike had been pulling a flagpole out of the ground when it hit a power line above his head and killed him instantly. The family asked if we would please come to their house, because they wanted to meet me—the girl Mike loved so much and talked about constantly.

I was devastated. I sobbed uncontrollably for hours and hours. Then I would sit for hours in shock. That evening, some of Mike's friends came and took us to his house. Although we met under such awful circumstances, I loved his family instantly; they were so warm and friendly, hugging me as we cried together. I remember sitting in his bedroom looking at a picture of me he had on his wall and letters I'd written him. I was in shock. I couldn't believe it.

The funeral services were a short time later. I stood by his casket, placing my hand on his and saw my picture in there with him. He had this leather bracelet he always wore, and his family gave it to me. I couldn't believe he was dead—even seeing him with my own eyes. I kept willing him to wake up, but he never did.

Afterward, I went home and listened to his voice on the answering machine about a billion times. My heart was broken. I didn't want to live anymore. I was in constant mourning for the boy I loved and the life I hoped we'd share together and couldn't stop crying. His family kept inviting me to do things with them, which was difficult as well, because I knew I'd never be part of them, and I loved them too. I thought my life was over, and I was destined to be this sad, pitiful individual for the rest of forever. I didn't want to love anyone else—I didn't want to move on—I only wanted him. Every day became bleaker and bleaker until I felt like I was going out of my mind.

One day I decided I'd had enough and needed to get away. I called my widowed grandma in another town and asked if I could come live with her and get a job there. My job transferred me to another store in her town, and my cousin and her father came and got me. I moved in with my grandma whom I loved dearly. And while I was happy to be surrounded by family I adored, I couldn't seem to get over my broken heart. I'd go to work, come home, and lie in bed crying for hours until I felt like I was going to be sick. I wished I could die too, just to escape the trauma going on inside me.

My cousin tried to help by setting me up on a date with another guy. By this time I was desperate for some kind of connection with anyone, so I agreed to go on a date with him, hoping it would help. He was a wonderful guy, and he really liked me . . . I liked him too, for that matter. There was definitely some chemistry between us, but every time I looked at him, I kept wishing he were Mike. I finally broke it off with him, feeling it was unfair to treat him the way I was. I've always regretted that relationship, because he really was wonderful. I guess I wasn't ready to let anyone in yet.

I continued on as I had been, working and crying, until one day another cousin, who was best friends with my mom, came and picked me up and took me out of the house for the day. She told me my grandma was worried about me, and it was time to let things go and move on with my life. I cried again, telling her I wasn't sure what to do. My heart hurt so badly. I agreed to enroll in some college classes and pursue my degree in music, which had been my original plan before I met Mike.

She took me home, and as I got out of the car, a couple of college guys drove by and honked the horn at me. I recognized them as a couple of boys who had dated friends of mine, and we'd become friends as well. My cousin asked me who they were, and I laughed and jokingly said, "Two guys I know, either of which I wouldn't mind dating." She smiled and said, "Maybe you should."

A couple of weeks later, while washing windows at work, a voice behind me said, "Well, hello there." I turned and saw James Weatherford, one of the two handsome guys who had honked at me. I smiled and gave him a hug. He told me he was there going to school and asked if I was too. I told him I planned on taking some music classes.

As luck would have it, my boss came and asked if I would like to go home early since things were slow. This surprised me because it never happened before. I agreed to leave but realized I'd carpooled and didn't have a way home. James offered me a ride and I ended up grocery shopping with him before he asked if I'd like to come watch a movie. I said I'd like that if he'd let me change my clothes first. I think my grandma was shocked when I told her I was going to hang out with a bunch of college guys.

And thus began the healing of my heart, as my once friend became my boyfriend. I loved the closeness we shared. He listened to me and held me through my tears over Mike—let me vent about it and get it out. He once said he felt like he'd won me by default. I told him that wasn't true because I'd been attracted to him before I met Mike and had wanted to date him, but it hadn't worked for us at the time.

At times I felt guilty for finding happiness again, I felt like I was betraying Mike's memory. It took a long time for me to realize that he loved me and would want me to be happy too. I married James six months later, and I knew with every breath I took, he was the love of my life.

It was many, many years later when the story for Chasing Nikki began to evolve in my mind. My mom had passed away suddenly from a massive pulmonary embolism after a fall. She was my best friend, and I found myself devastated by heartbreak once again. I wasn't sure how I'd ever live without her. Our family learned a lot about blood clots the hard way, and I began to hear numerous stories of people whose lives had been affected by similar tragedies. I was determined to draw attention to this silent killer and make people aware of the dangers, hoping to prevent this horror in the lives of others.

I met Chase Walden a short time later and was very impressed by him. I asked him if he would be a part of this project—a retelling of bits and pieces of my story, but wrapped around pieces of him as the main character. He readily agreed, and I was thrilled. I carefully wove real parts of him throughout the story, sometimes mirroring events in his life without even knowing. That was an interesting experience, but since those things are personal to him I won't share them, but suffice it to say he was a huge inspiration to me.

It has been a very tearful journey to get to this point, but I think writing these books has been very therapeutic as well. Who knows why things happen the way they do, but I honestly believe I was meant to share this story. I hope, on some level, it resonated well with you.

Love Conquers All,
Lacey

12 Fun Real Facts About My Muse Chase:

He is an honest-to-goodness, freaking ridiculously amazing quarterback. Remember the name, people. You *will* hear it in the NFL someday!

He wears the number 23 jersey.

He drives a white Dodge truck.

White is actually his favorite color.

He loves beta fish and likes to sing to them. And yes, he now has one named Turk.

He works with horses (and a huge ole scary bull with ginormous horns) in a big red barn on his stepdad's ranch.

He likes to camp and fish.

Little kids love him.

He loves his mom.

Yes, he's got the muscles going on too (though he likes to tell me how fat he is at times, which usually gets him a well deserved eye roll).

While he's known for his sexy swagger and broody good looks, he can be very funny with a quick humor that hits you unexpectedly and makes you laugh out loud.

He came up with the ideas for the cover photo shoot, and I think he did an amazing job.

About the Author

Lacey Weatherford is the bestselling author of many young adult books such as the Of Witches and Warlocks series, and Crush. She has always loved books and wanted to become a writer since reading her first Nancy Drew novel at the age of eight.

Lacey resides in the beautiful White Mountains of Arizona. She lives with her wonderful husband, children, and their family pets. When she's not out supporting one of her kids at their sporting/music events, she spends her time reading, writing, blogging, and socializing with her readers on her social media accounts.

Visit Lacey's Official Website:
www.laceyweatherfordbooks.com
Follow on Twitter:
LMWeatherford
Or Facebook:
Lacey Jackson Weatherford
Or
Lacey Weatherford- Author

Other Books by Lacey Weatherford:

Of Witches and Warlocks series
The Trouble with Spells
The Demon Kiss
Blood of the White Witch
The Dark Rising
Possession of Souls

Chasing Nikki series
Chasing Nikki

Crush series
Crush

Multi-author Anthology
A Midsummer Night's Fling

Also from
Moonstruck Media

Would love
be enough?

Broken
PROMISES

Belinda Boring

Book One in the Brianna Lane series

What would you do if the man you loved became one of your greatest enemies? Would your love be enough to save him?

All Bri wanted to do was spend her Friday night with the man she loved and adored. Little did she know leaving her home would result in her relationship with Quinn being tested beyond its limits.

Fae have been organizing to invade Earth, and their devious plans are culminating now, colliding with Bri's very existence. Using a powerful glamour, the Fae trigger each person's violent tendencies, turning the streets into a battleground and strangers against each other. In a crushing blow, Quinn becomes affected and Bri finds herself battling to save her lover from himself as he stalks her relentlessly, taunting her at every turn.

But fighting for her love isn't her only worry. As the battle ensues, Bri discovers a startling truth about her own heritage that she must come to terms with. She has no other choice but to fight, leading her to a confrontation that will change her world forever - and threaten to leave her with broken promises.

DEENA REMIEL

DEVIL DU JOUR

THE BOOK WAITRESS SERIES

Book two in the highly acclaimed Book Waitress series from bestselling author, Deena Remiel!

The Book Waitress, Camille Dutton, has luck on her side. Good and bad. On the upside, she narrowly escaped death and Satan claiming her soul. On the downside, a portal has been opened, and she can feel every time a creature from Hell crosses over to our world.

Derek Galloway is one tenacious man. His curious nature won't let him rest until he closes Hell's portal and finds a cure for Camille's affliction. Satan will have one helluva fight on his hands if he tries to claim her again.

Camille and Derek, an unlikely couple, have found each other in the darkest of times. Will they find the answers they need to free her and the world from Satan's grip? Or are they in for the longest, darkest battle of their lives?

The God Chronicles

Zeus

Kamery Solomon

Book one in The God Chronicles: Zeus, from bestselling author, Kamery Solomon, coming soon!

Vegas is not where Karly had imagined herself to be at this point in her life. She was supposed to be living in California, soaking up the sun and enjoying the life of an artist. Instead, she's just moving out of her parents and going to a school that could loosely be called her second choice.

When she meets Zeus Drakos, owner of the new hit casino and resort in town, he seems just like every other jerk guy out there. How was she supposed to know he was the exiled god of Mt. Olympus?

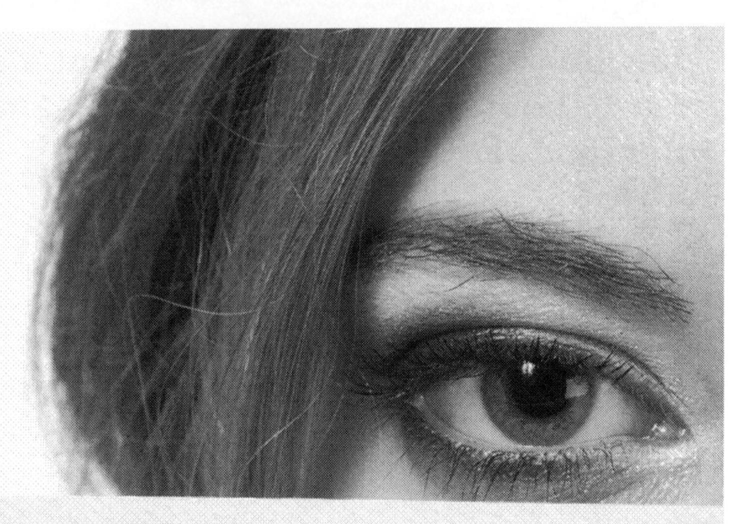

"She thought she was all alone...he proved her wrong."

Saving Me

KELSIE BLANTON

Saving Me, a young adult contemporary novel from new author, Kelsie Blanton, coming soon!

16 year old Peyton Jones had it all: straight A's in school, the perfect boyfriend, and nothing to worry about but keeping her GPA up. Then one night it's suddenly ripped away from her. Everything she has ever known changes and she goes from having a perfect plan to watching her world crumble around her.

Steve Gibbons was the quarterback of his high school football team...until the new guy showed up and stole his spot, causing him to lose his chance at a scholarship.
Football was his life and now he feels like he has nothing.

Drawn together after losing hope for their futures, Peyton and Steve become best friends, but as they grow closer something happens that changes everything. Will Peyton be left to face things alone, or can she trust enough to let someone else in?

Printed in Great Britain
by Amazon.co.uk, Ltd.,
Marston Gate.